One Fin

CU00588949

ABIGAIL SHIRLEY

Dedicated to Nan, who also loved writing. She would have been proud that there was a writer in the family after all.

FOREWORD

On April 23rd 2009 my husband, Jordan, and I left our home in Cornwall, England bound for Nicaragua, Central America. With just one suitcase each in hand and return tickets set for six months later, we were embarking on an adventure of a lifetime. We had spent months planning and preparing and now we were off to spend an extended period of time in this poor country working as volunteers.

The excitement and anticipation I felt that day gave no warning of the intense homesickness I found myself suffering with for the first few months after we arrived in Nicaragua. I cried most days and felt generally miserable. The strangest part was not that I longed for Cornwall so much, but that I missed Banbury, the town where I grew up with my family. Banbury was the town I had left some five years earlier. It seemed that the feelings I felt were more than homesickness; it was a 'childhood' sickness. All the things and places I was longing for were from my childhood.

It was during this time that I started to write 'One Fine Lady.' I sat one afternoon in my hammock and wrote chapter one. The next day I completed chapter two. Then I read these two chapters to Jordan. "What do you think?" I asked. "I like it," he replied. "You should make this your project, try and finish it."

And that's just what I did. I researched the fascinating history of my home town with its canal and cross. I included as many real life places as I could. And I wrote about the things I missed from home, particularly from my childhood; those evening walks by the canal, paddling in the brook by Bodicote and blackberry picking. Subconsciously I aged Becky at the age I always want to go back to when life gets too much. And 12/13 seemed more appropriate for the activities that young Becky would enjoy.

Soon I settled in Nicaragua and it became our home for almost two years. Consequently, I wasn't so desperate to write about England. Then, once we had returned to British life the hustle and bustle took over. My story, Becky's story, remained half written for a few years. Now finally I have completed it, just as Jordan had said I should do.

"Ride a cock horse to Banbury
Cross

To see a fine lady upon a
white horse

With rings on her fingers and
bells on her toes

She shall have music
wherever she goes"

(unknown)

1

1860

<u>Spring</u>

1

"Oh, thank goodness!" Becky thought to herself. "I should make it there just in time."

With a pace somewhere between a jog and a walk the young girl turned about and quickly made her way along the narrow tow path and back towards the red-bricked arch bridge, which she had just moments earlier crossed over. Every few steps she added a little skip as she hurriedly manoeuvred her way around the green hedgerows that were fast sprouting both upwards and outwards at the side of the tow path. Upon reaching the underneath of the arch bridge she crouched down, catching her breath, and sighed gently in relief.

Looking to her side she could see that the sky, which had only a few minutes earlier been as blue as the little girl's eyes, was now rapidly clouding over and she was sure that a heavy rain shower was heading in her direction.

As her beating heart steadily slowed and her breathing gradually returned to normal, the first heavy drops of rain began to land on the thick wooden planks above her head. She let out another satisfied sigh, glad that she had taken the initiative to turn around and run for cover. Beneath the bridge, the young girl started to make herself and the awkwardly shaped bundle that she was carrying comfortable as she leaned back against the cool sloping brick wall.

"Now, now. Settle down," she whispered softly into the heap of material that was held in her arms. "Stop wriggling in there, it's okay now."

Becky was clutching, tightly against her chest, a wrapped-up bundle of old rags. Movement was coming from inside the material and the small girl was struggling to hold it still.

"Well that settles it... I'll just have to call you Fidget!" she said cheerfully. "Yes, that's a perfect name. Now where are you? Oh, here you are."

As she carefully pulled the pieces of fabric apart, Becky grinned down at the small, black and white face which was looking back at her.

"So that's settled then.... How do you do Fidget?"

Almost as if acknowledging this rather formal greeting, the little kitten waved his tiny white paw out from underneath the rags and tried to catch a strand of the girl's hair that was gently swaying back and forth while she leaned over to stroke him.

"Hee, hee!" she giggled. "You're a cheeky fella' aren't ya'?"

The thick, dark clouds were directly overhead now and giant, heavy drops of rain were rapidly splashing down, landing onto the wooden bridge. Within a short time some of the rain drops began to fall through the gaps in the wooden planks above where the little girl and the kitten were sheltering. As one big droplet landed heavily on Fidget's small, black nose, Becky smiled to herself and started to lovingly wrap the little kitten back up, into the bundle of rags.

"Don't worry, it will soon pass. It's only a spring shower. I'll have you home in no time."

Becky was right. Remarkably, after just ten minutes, the black rain clouds cleared away towards the horizon and the sun was shining brightly again. She stood up, a little stiffly from crouching down but still holding tightly to the wrapped up kitten, and looked around. Behind her, in the distance, she could see a beautiful rainbow stretching out across the sky.

"Hopefully someone in Kings Sutton village has found a pot of gold," she thought to herself and then turned to continue on her way home.

Just another half a mile along the canal tow path and Becky could see the grey outline of the industrial buildings that were situated on the outskirts of Banbury town. Only another ten minutes down the canal was home.

As Becky approached the old stone lockhouse the setting sun was casting long, dark shadows across the still water in the canal. Becky could see Mr Dickenson shutting up the coal shed that lay opposite the house and she called out a cheery greeting to him.

"Well. Hello there Miss Becky," he replied. "I didn't realise you weren't home yet. Have you been to see your friend, Miss Amy?"

"Yes. I have," she answered.

Mr Dickenson had lived opposite Becky and her father for as long as she could remember. He had known Becky's father for a very long time and had watched her grow over the years. Quite a tall man, with greying hair, he had a quiet and gentle personality. Mr Dickenson bought coal from the docks in London and then had it delivered all over the town.

"Is Father here?" Becky asked, glancing over at the lockhouse.

"I think he's out back," Mr Dickenson paused and then added. "Feeding your chickens..."

"Oh dear!" sighed Becky. "I was supposed to do that before it got dark. I'd better hurry in. Goodnight Mr Dickenson,"

"Night duckie. See you tomorrow." The old man went in and turned to close the shed door behind him. He smiled as he watched the young girl run towards the canal. She was growing up fast and yet it still showed how young she was with her careless, forgetful ways. Closing the door to, he hoped that Jim Bailey had had a good day, for the child's sake.

Becky made her way quickly across the canal towards the lockhouse. It was a small stone house, just to the north of the lock, set only a couple of yards back from the tow path.

~~~~

Becky's father had worked lock number twenty nine in

Banbury for thirty years. He had started working there with old Mr Thomas in 1830 when he was just thirteen years old. Becky's mother had worked alongside her sister, Rose, in the kitchens of the Whately Coaching Inn from the age of fourteen until she was married. Jim Bailey married Becky's mother when he was twenty two years old. A year later Mr Thomas died, leaving Jim Bailey to continue working the lock and to live in the house with his young wife. Seven years later, in the late August of 1847, after several miscarriages, Becky was born in that same house. Jim Bailey doted on his wife, Myriam, and their beautiful baby girl. Always a glint in his eye, he was one of the most cheerful and most liked workmen in the town. Sadly though, his beloved wife never recovered from the complications of Becky's birth and gradually her body became weaker and weaker until one hot summer day, when Becky was almost three years old, she died peacefully at home, in her husband's arms.

Jim Bailey's world fell apart. He closed himself off from everyone around him, especially from those who reminded him of Myriam. The glint he had once held in his eye was now replaced by a vacant, sorrowful expression. Unable to handle his huge loss and his intense grief, he could no longer cope with life or the child that was left in his care. With feelings of love for the happiness she had brought, yet bitterness for the deep sadness that had followed, he lost all ability to extend any emotion towards anything or anyone, especially towards her. Jim Bailey and his daughter, Rebecca, had lived for almost a decade as acquaintances sharing the same house; one desperately reaching out for love and the other unable to give it.

~~~~

Becky hurriedly made her way through a small wooden gate, at the side of the house that led into the cottage garden beyond. Through the evening dusk, she could see that her father was down the end, by the wall, putting the hens in the coop for the night. Carefully tucking the precious bundle that she was carrying under one arm she took a cup with her free hand, scooped into it some grain and then made her way down, past the vegetables, to join her father.

"I'm sorry Father," she said, sprinkling the grain into the coop. "I meant to get back earlier. It's just; there was a shower, a heavy one. It's April now you know."

Still not having turned around, he began closing the door on the coop.

"Anyway, I have a surprise," continued Becky. "We won't have to worry about the mice and rats any more!" She paused, holding her breath as her father turned to face her.

"Look what Mr Haynes has given us!"

Having put the cup down, she unfolded the bundle of rags and held Fidget out high for her father to see. "Amy saved this one just for me. He was the fattest!"

Jim Bailey looked slowly and deliberately from the kitten to his daughter, and then back to the kitten again.

"He doesn't look capable of catching a grasshopper,"

he mumbled.

"He's still only a baby, Father," Becky replied. "He'll soon grow though," she added eagerly.

As Becky looked up, hopefully at her father, willing him to say she could keep the kitten, a faint and almost pathetic 'miaow' came from Fidget's mouth. In response the deeply engrained frown lines on Jim Bailey's forehead slowly faded a little and the corners of his mouth rose slightly in a sort of half smile. Not sure what this strange expression on her father's face meant; Becky again held her breath while Fidget punched a small white paw into the air and made the same noise again, only this time a little louder. Stepping towards the pair and gently rubbing the kitten's head with his fingertips, Jim Bailey felt an odd, warmth come over him. It was a strange feeling, one that he hadn't felt for a long time.

"You've got a bit of character haven't you?" he said, still stroking the kitten's head.

Becky's eyes widened as she stared nervously at her father. She didn't know if this unfamiliar behaviour was good or bad.

Suddenly aware of the child that was looking up at him; Jim Bailey hastily lowered his hand and turned towards the lockhouse.

"You're late and I'm hungry now."

"Oh, it's okay," said Becky. "Mrs Haynes gave me chicken pie. It's here in my bag."

"Well that's one thing you've done right," he replied, now entering the doorway at the back of the cottage which led directly into the kitchen.

"But Father?" Becky hesitated. "What about the kitten?"

Jim Bailey lit the lamp and disappeared behind the door. "Just keep him out of my way," he replied. Then he returned to the doorway and looked down the garden at her. "Now hurry up Rebecca," he demanded. "I want my dinner!"

2

Daily life for twelve year old Rebecca Bailey was fairly routine and largely uneventful. Each morning, as the sun began to rise up over the fields surrounding Banbury, she would get up and out of her bed, start the fire in the kitchen stove and then prepare a good breakfast for her father.

From early on after his wife's death Jim Bailey made it clear that he had no time to 'care for' the child. Myriam's older sister, Rose Watkins, lived in the town and from the start took the small child under her wing, while providing for many of her widowed brother-in-law's needs. As Becky grew she had to learn, far sooner than other girls her age, how to keep a house. Aunt Rosa (Becky's affectionate name for her) spent many hours over the years teaching the small innocent child the correct way to clean dishes, light the stove and cook a few simple meals. The result was that now, at just twelve years of age, Becky could capably run the home.

Jim Bailey worked hard all day collecting tolls, checking water levels and opening and closing the large heavy wooden gates of the lock for those who passed through. He needed plenty of energy to keep him going right through until evening. Becky usually cooked up a few eggs for breakfast together with some fresh bread and sometimes added a little meat, if left over from the previous evening, to go along with it.

During the colder wintry months, Becky would then rake out the large open fireplace in the lounge and clean up the pale grey ash left over from the night before. She would then lay pieces of dry, neatly cut kindling in the fireplace, ready for the evening. Once her father had finished his breakfast Becky would clear the plates and breakfast things away before going outside to deal with the chickens. Chickens are dirty creatures and the coop where they spent the night needed cleaning daily. Becky had given all six chickens individual names and she would usually chatter away to them while sweeping up the mess from inside the coop. Becky's morning jobs finished when she collected up any eggs that had been laid during the previous night and placed them in a small basket that sat on the kitchen table. From that moment, until Becky began to cook the evening dinner, the day was free for whatever she wanted.

Jim Bailey was not a rich man yet neither was he a pauper. Although he could afford to, it had never occurred to him that he might send his child to school. So Becky spent most of her time beside the lock, talking to the many people that passed by. Sometimes she was able to sell some eggs or a jar of chutney that she had made to the families that lived on the canal. The part of the canal that ran through Banbury was a regular journey for many of the men who drove the boats along with their wives and children and Becky made friends with most of the families that passed through. From time to time she was able to see other places if they invited her to hop onto the boat for a while.

On a Monday morning she helped Betty, whose

husband was manager in the nearby stables, while she did their washing for the week. This was a luxury that Jim Bailey was willing to pay for as he had no idea of how to go about cleaning clothes and bed sheets. Added to that, Becky was not a particularly big girl for her age and when left to wash out sheets alone, she tended to drop parts on the ground and the material would end up dirtier than when she began. So each week Betty, a slight but strong young woman, spent a few hours washing out and drying their things.

On Thursdays Becky would sometimes go to the market close to the town centre. Her best friend, Amy, and her family often brought animals and produce to sell there and Becky loved wandering around, looking at all the bustling stalls, different animals and various goings on.

From time to time, Becky would walk up through the town to the Whately Coaching Inn. Aunt Rosa worked in the kitchens there and often saved Becky some of the leftovers from lunch. Becky loved spending time with her aunt. She would sit the girl down with a cup of hot tea and tell her stories about her mother. Becky always felt a warm radiance glowing in her heart each time her Aunt Rosa hugged her tight when they said goodbye.

One quiet Wednesday morning Becky was sitting on the verge next to the stony tow path, a few yards down from the lock, playing with Fidget. He had been with them for almost a week and was settling in well. Becky had lovingly knitted a toy mouse and was patiently trying to teach the energetic kitten to hunt. Whilst they were playing, fast flowing ripples started to rush across the surface of the water next to where Becky sat. The ripples were coming from the lock as it was being emptied, and Becky looked up to see who was coming through.

Stood by the lock, talking to her father was Mr Hardy. Isabelle, his three year old daughter, was stood holding tightly onto his hand. As she stared with her wide brown eyes at the water that was rapidly disappearing from the lock she gently sucked the thumb of her free hand.

Ron Hardy, his wife and Isabelle lived just up the canal and sold timber. Boats were always coming and going from their yard, making deliveries all around but Mr Hardy never normally drove them himself. He had four boatmen working for him and they made all the deliveries.

Becky was curious about why Mr Hardy was driving the boat. Then, as she was sat watching the two men talking, her father looked around. When he spotted where Becky was sitting he beckoned for her to come over to join them.

Becky was small for her age. She had big blue eyes and shoulder length, mousey brown hair that was partially covered by a white bonnet. Her complexion was clear and pale, much like fine porcelain and although she was often outside, the sun never really altered her skin tone a great deal. She was wearing a simple blue, gingham dress. Being a shy girl in plain clothes she often went unnoticed by many. Those who stopped to talk to her though, discovered that as they looked deeper she possessed a calm, serene beauty. It was a

13

beauty that would blossom as she grew older.

She immediately got up, and obediently made her way over to the lock, with Fidget jumping and pouncing after her ankles.

"Rebecca," said her father, "Ron here has got to return this boat to his brother. He is taking it through to Aynho. Elizabeth is looking after the yard so he's got young Isabelle here too."

Becky waved at the little girl who had turned her gaze away from the canal and was now watching the energetic kitten as it leapt all around them. With tight curls in her dark-brown hair and wearing a beautiful lilac dress, she was still sucking her thumb.

"The thing is Becky," said Mr Hardy, "Isabelle can be a handful. I was wondering if you could come along with me and keep her occupied."

"Of course," smiled Becky. She loved the opportunity to go out on the canal. Although Becky was good at keeping herself entertained, she did become tired of her own company. Any chance to spend a bit of time with other people was welcomed eagerly.

"Just move that animal out of my way before you leave," ordered Jim Bailey and Becky picked Fidget up and quickly put him inside the house, away from where her father was working.

After the boat had been pushed out of the lock and Blackie, Mr Hardy's great big Shire horse who usually worked in his yard, had been hitched up to the front, Becky climbed onto the boat and sat up on top. Mr

Hardy lifted Isabelle up to the roof next to Becky and he went to the back in order to steer the rudder. Ben Coleman, who worked for Mr Hardy, then started to lead Blackie forwards along the tow path and they were on their way.

"Bye Father. See you later," called Becky. Jim Bailey was closing the gate on the lock and without even looking up he briefly held one hand up above his head as a farewell.

It wasn't hard to keep Isabelle occupied as they made their way down the canal. Having no brothers or sisters of her own she enjoyed the attention that Becky gave her.

Not far out of Banbury, Becky looked ahead and spotted that one of the numerous swing bridges was down, over the canal.

"Come on Isabelle, I'll show you how to lift the bridge up."

Becky jumped down, off the slow moving boat and held her arms up to the little girl. Isabelle was a little frightened of the moving boat and looked over at her father. Mr Hardy had been watching and he stepped out onto the tow path, walked along to where his daughter was sitting and then lifted her down to the ground beside Becky. He returned to the back of the boat and the two girls ran off together down the tow path to the bridge. Stamping her feet on the wooden planks of the bridge, Isabelle waved fervidly to the barge that was making its way towards them. Mr Hardy chuckled and waved back to her.

15

On the other side of the canal Becky stood underneath one of the two big wooden arms that went from the base of the bridge and then extended up steeply into the air. Jumping as high as she could, she still couldn't reach it. Isabelle came and stood next to her. She then also started jumping up and down alongside Becky.

"Good effort you two!" The boat had now reached the bridge and Ben was walking towards the two girls.

"I bet you can't reach it either," said Becky, slightly embarrassed that she couldn't lift the bridge up. She had seen some of the tall farmers do it effortlessly many times and thought it was easy.

"No. I can't reach it. I'm not tall enough. However, unlike you I'm heavy enough," Ben replied.

Ben was eighteen years old and moving timber around all day had given him a muscular build. He jumped onto one of the thick wooden arms and started to climb up it. When he was just past halfway along the arm his weight began to counterbalance that of the bridge and it started to lift up into the air behind him. Suddenly the two heavy wooden arms dropped and slammed down onto the ground knocking Ben off and onto the grass. Jumping up quickly, Ben then secured one of the arms with a chain. The bridge was now open for Mr Hardy to take Blackie and the boat through.

Ben stood grinning cheekily at Becky while Isabelle paused, wide-eyed, staring at the bridge with her thumb firmly in her mouth. Then, her eyes filling up with tears, she turned to Becky and started crying.

"Oh, it's alright Isabelle. It just made a big bang, that's all. Everyone's okay." Becky lifted the little girl up into her arms. "We're going to close the bridge now and get back on the boat with daddy."

Ben gently lowered the bridge and Becky started to walk back across to continue along the tow path but the little girl in her arms started screaming and wriggling to get down.

Becky looked at Ben. "I think I'll have to walk along the fields this side until we get to the arch bridge. She's too scared of this bridge now."

Lowering the frightened little girl to the ground and taking her hand Becky started walking along the field on the opposite side of the tow path. Within a few minutes Isabelle had forgotten all about the scary swing bridge. There were too many other interesting things to see. It was springtime and the countryside all around the canal was coming to life. Bees and dragonflies were busy doing their work and many of the fields had young lambs in them, all skipping about in the sunshine. The two girls were walking along at about the same pace as the boat on the canal and Isabelle kept calling out to her father, pointing out various things that she could see.

As they approached the arch bridge where Becky had sheltered from the rain not too many evenings before, Isabelle tugged Becky's arm and pointed up to the top of the field. Slowly making their way down the hill was a small herd of dairy cows followed by a boy.

Becky smiled and called out, "David! Hey. David! It's me, Becky."

The boy waved both hands in the air and continued driving the cows down towards the canal. As he got closer to the bridge he shouted, "Becky! Open the gate on the other side, will you?"

She ran to open the gate and as the cows came over the bridge they made their way into the field beyond and began grazing. Becky turned around and faced David.

"Well now Rebecca Bailey, what are you doing here? Not looking for another kitten I hope!"

He gave her a soft punch on the arm and waved to Mr Hardy who was waiting on the other side of the bridge.

"No. Mr Hardy is taking his boat to Aynho and he asked me to come along and look after Isabelle."

"Well I never. Just a few weeks ago and there I was babysitting you and my little sister. Now look how grown up you are! Well you must excuse me *Lady Rebecca*." He held his hand out to her and then started laughing.

"Ha ha. You're so funny!" she replied, pretending to be annoyed.

David was the older brother of Amy Haynes, Becky's best friend. The family owned a small farm up on the hill just a couple of miles outside of Banbury. David was fifteen, nearly three years older than Becky, and he stood towering over the little girl. Being a farmer's son he was strong for his age. His skin was already tanned brown and his thick hair bronzed yellow from working out of doors.

"Have you just finished milking the cows?" asked Becky.

"Yes. We are getting quite fast at it now. Father will probably start buying some more cows soon."

The once booming wool trade that had provided Banbury, and the Haynes family, with a steady income for many decades was now slowly grinding to a halt. Only a few factories were still open and buyers were becoming hard to find. Samuel Haynes and his wife Mary were making changes to their farm to counteract the decline in the wool trade. They were investing in dairy cows and it seemed as though things were working well for them.

David gave a distracted glance up the hill, towards the farm. "I'm sorry folks but I can't stop and chat all day. I've got to get to my lessons."

Mr Haynes wanted his son to be a clever farmer. A farmer who would be able to use his brain and work his way out of a crisis if ever he encountered one. So two mornings a week David attended lessons in the nearby village of Bodicote run by the voluntary Church Society.

David nodded to Mr Hardy and Ben, flashed a quick grin at Becky and then set off back up the hill.

"David..." Becky called after him.

"Don't worry Lady Rebecca. I'll tell my sister that I've seen you," he shouted back to her.

Becky took Isabelle's hand and they ran alongside the canal to catch up with Mr Hardy who was already continuing along his way. Just a few hours and a couple of locks later they reached the wharf at Aynho. The small village of Aynho sat on top of a hill and the canal snaked around the base and then continued to Oxford where it joined the Thames and went all the way to London.

The Wharf was alive with the activity of people loading and unloading their narrow boats and barges so Becky took Isabelle and led her and Blackie off to a quiet corner, leaving Mr Hardy and Ben to sort the barge out. Becky showed Isabelle how to wipe the hot, sweaty horse down, give him some water, a few handfuls of fresh sweet grass and a peppermint to eat. The little girl squealed in delight as Blackie's big, wet tongue licked all over her small hand.

After a while Mr Hardy and Ben came over to where the two girls were sat making daisy chains and Mr Hardy said that it was time to go.

"Boat...Daddy. Can we go on the boat?" asked Isabelle and pointed to the boats and barges all lined up by the loading bay.

"No dear. Blackie is going to take us home tonight," he turned to Becky. "I only borrowed the boat off my brother while one of mine was getting fixed at Tooley's boatyard. Mine went back into the water today so I've returned Bill's one as I don't need it any more. It just means there is no boat to take us home. So it looks like you two are on Blackie."

Mr Hardy lifted the two girls up onto the big black horse and they all set off back down the tow path. Ben walked quickly on ahead, eager to get home, while Mr Hardy led Blackie gently along the path. Isabelle was tired from the day's excitements and soon fell asleep, leaning back against Becky.

"Poor little thing. She's had a long day," said Becky.

"Yes, a long and exciting day," replied Mr Hardy. "She doesn't often get to go out and see so much wildlife." He paused, thoughtfully. Then, making a short 'tutting' sound, he continued, "maybe as she gets older I'll stop being so protective and let her wander around a bit more."

"I wouldn't worry too much, Mr Hardy, about keeping her near to you. I like seeing how close you two are," said Becky. She finished speaking and then stared intently at the strand of black mane that she was holding onto, hoping desperately that he wouldn't notice the sadness in her voice.

He turned his head around and looked at her. "I'm sorry Becky. I forget myself. Things have been hard for you. Not just that, for your father too. Your mother would be proud to see what a fine young lady you are becoming and I'm sure that your father is too...even if he doesn't find words to say it."

She looked back at him and forced a smile.

"Maybe."

21

But she sounded far from convinced.

As they approached the arch bridge in an awkward silence a figure stood up, from where it had been sitting on the bridge, and started waving frantically to them, calling out, "Becky?! Rebecca Bailey is that you?"

Mr Hardy saw a genuine smile now appear on Becky's face. "It's my friend, Amy," she explained. "David must have told her that we would be coming back past. Could you wave to her for me, please? I don't want to disturb Isabelle."

By the time they reached the bridge Amy was jumping up and down all over the place. Only nine months older than Becky she was an excitable teenager. Wearing a simple cotton dress with her long blonde hair tied back in a ribbon she stood on the bridge with a grin that looked just as cheeky as that of her brother's.

"Oh Becky. I've been waiting here for days!" she exaggerated. "I'm *so* excited!"

Becky started to giggle at her friend's funny behaviour.

"Don't laugh at me," she said still jumping up and down. "I'm excited because I've got good news, the best news....Mother said that you can stay for the night! Father even said that we can sleep in the barn!"

Becky gave a small squeal of delight.

Amy continued, "You can stay the night, we can sleep in the barn and then you can come into town with us tomorrow when we go to the market."

As Amy was speaking Becky's smile started to disappear.

"But Amy, I can't," she sighed. "It's Father... well, you know."

Amy looked at her triumphantly. "No Becky. I have arranged everything. Mother has made a chicken and mushroom pie and I collected some bread and jam for his breakfast tomorrow. It's all here in this basket, if Mr Hardy doesn't mind taking it."

Becky's smile returned again. "Oh, well done Amy. What a good idea!" she looked at Mr Hardy. "Would you mind if I left you here and went with Amy?"

"Not at all," he replied. "It sounds like you two are going to have fun. And don't worry; I'll give the things to your father. He'll be fine. You go on and enjoy yourself."

"Thank you Mr Hardy. Could you just ask Father to give a little bit of the mushroom sauce to Fidget, the kitten?"

"Of course," he replied, "and thank you for your help with Isabelle today."

Ron Hardy climbed onto the wall of the bridge and helped to carefully lift Becky down from the horse. They both tried as best they could to prevent Isabelle from waking and, although she stirred a little, once Mr Hardy was up on Blackie and sat behind her she again fell into a restful sleep. Becky jumped softly from the wall to the ground and then passed the basket of food from Amy up to him. With a nudge from the man's heels, Blackie began walking forwards again, away from the bridge and towards home. The sun was now setting behind the fields and the dispersing rays of light were spreading pastel colours out across the water. Blackie and his two riders began to blend into the dark shadows of the hedgerow as they continued down the tow path. The two friends stood on the bridge waving goodbye. Then, linking arms, they turned and made their way up the hill, away from the canal.

3

It didn't worry Jim Bailey that his daughter was spending the night with Samuel Haynes and his family. He knew that she would be excited and talkative about her journey to Aynho Wharf and it always made him feel uneasy whenever she wanted to chatter to him. He preferred not to have her disturbing and bothering him. Besides, Mary Haynes baked a good pie and when he finished work in the evening the only thing that concerned Jim Bailey was that he had a full stomach.

It was already dark when Jim Bailey fed the chickens and shut them in the coop for the night. He then went indoors to wash up for tea.

Although he found it hard to cope with the noise that his daughter made around him, he found it harder still to deal with the now silent house. Silence was a painful reminder that Myriam was no longer there and the darkness of night-time highlighted his loneliness.

Before settling down to enjoy the chicken pie he lit the fire. It wasn't a cold evening but he hoped that the sound of the hot logs crackling in the fireplace would disguise the silence that surrounded him.

Just as he started to tuck into the delicious pie he heard a faint 'miaow.' The hungry little kitten came into the room and lay down in front of the fireplace, rolling around on his back. Jim Bailey grunted to himself. He wasn't in the mood to have the young animal chasing around and jumping all over his feet. Then he remembered that Rebecca had sent a message asking him to give the kitten some food. Letting out a sigh of annoyance he got up and fetched a small plate from the kitchen and then spooned a little of the creamy mushroom filling from the pie onto it. After placing the plate on the floor in front of the fire he continued with his own meal.

Just as he was finishing the last piece of pastry crust Jim Bailey heard a strange noise. It was like a low, faint rumble of thunder. Surprised, he looked around and shortly realized that this noise was coming from the kitten. Fidget had finished his mushroom sauce and was lying outstretched by the roaring fire licking his paws clean. He felt warm, well-fed and content and so was purring gently.

Jim Bailey grunted again to himself and thought about shoving the animal outside but instead he settled back down into his armchair. The warmth from the fire and the kitten's soft purring gradually caused his eyelids to grow heavy. A few moments later and he fell fast asleep. There they both stayed until daybreak. One lay on the floor purring contentedly, the other slumped in the chair snoring peacefully.

4

On market mornings the countryside around Banbury, and its inhabitants, arose early and this Thursday was no exception. David burst noisily into the barn at five o'clock to wake the two young girls who were wrapped up in blankets, fast asleep on top of the hay stacks.

"Come on," he said, shaking each of them. "Its milking time. Wake up!"

"Hey. Stop shaking me. I'm awake!" shouted Amy, trying to punch and kick her brother to get him off her. She wasn't really a morning person and didn't much like his way of waking her up.

"Mooooo!" he continued and gave her a sharp poke in the ribs.

Amy's face turned red with annoyance. She had had enough. Leaping out from under the blanket, she chased him out of the barn and into the yard. Giggling to herself Becky got up and went to join them. The early morning air was still cool and she shivered a little.

Even though the sun was still fast asleep and had not yet come up over the horizon, a few lanterns enabled Becky to see that the farmyard was already alive with activity. Mr Haynes had been down to the bottom field and driven the Friesian cows up to the farm. Now the large, black and white beasts were milling around the yard, with heavy udders, waiting to go into the shed for milking.

"Stop fooling around now you two," ordered Mr Haynes, leading the first Friesian into the milking shed. "The quicker we get this done, the quicker we can all get into town."

David stopped teasing his sister and started to lead the second Friesian into the shed. "Come on you two. Grab a cow!" he called to the two girls as they stood watching, Amy rearranging her hair, which had been ruffled up during her wrestle with David.

Normally they only had two stations set up inside the shed for milking but today Mr Haynes had set up a third. The previous evening Becky, who was usually so quiet, had asked many questions about the Hayneses' new line of business and Samuel Haynes thought that she might enjoy having a go.

Amy helped her friend to tie the cow up and showed her where to place the empty pail. She then explained how to move her fingers around the udders to get the milk out. At first Becky couldn't do it, and her forehead furrowed into a worried frown. Then slowly, as she began to get used to it, her pail gradually began to fill with warm frothy milk and she started to smile happily.

Nearly an hour later, after Mr Haynes had milked three cows and David had done two, Becky was just about finishing her second pail. David came over to see how she was getting on.

"Do you think you've made her sore yet?!" he asked with a teasing glint in his eye.

Still smiling yet not turning her head away from the work that her hands were doing, Becky replied, "You can tease me all you like, but I don't care. This is the most fun I've had for ages."

"Well I'm glad to hear it. Young girls like you and my sister should be having fun."

Although Becky was always happy when she was with her friend Amy and they spent a lot of time playing like little girls, David knew that her home life wasn't quite the same. Being the older brother of the young girl's best friend he felt that it was his duty to look out for her. Giving her a pat on the shoulders he turned and started moving the urns of milk out of the shed.

Once the milking was over Mr Haynes told David to put the cows into the top field, nearest to the farmyard. "There's no time to walk them all the way down to the bottom," he said, "they'll be fine up here for today."

The girls went inside the farmhouse to wash up for breakfast. Becky enjoyed mealtimes with Amy and her family. There was always a cheerful sound of happy conversation around the table. Unused to the lively atmosphere, Becky would often sit just looking from person to person while they told each other all about the activities they had been involved in. But today was different. Becky had enjoyed the new experience in the milking shed and she was eager to talk about it.

As Becky chattered away, explaining to Mrs Haynes exactly just how difficult it was to milk a cow, Samuel Haynes looked across the table at his wife and raised his eyebrows. Mary Haynes smiled back at her husband and nodded her head in agreement with his unsaid thoughts. They were both very fond of their daughter's little friend and it made them happy to see her coming out of herself in this way.

By half past eight they were all outside and ready to go to the market. Mr Haynes had loaded two rams into the cart and had hitched Daisy, the horse, up to it. There was also a small trailer cart attached at the back full of cabbages, leeks, cheese, butter and two large churns of fresh milk. As they made their way along the lane towards Banbury they joined many other farmers and their families all off to the market.

The market was an important part of the town's life. Families like the Hayneses, who spent their days working hard on the land around the town, had a chance to earn some money while those who worked in the industries belonging to the town had a chance to buy their necessary provisions. Banbury was a well-established market town. The town not only boasted a large cattle market but also a corn, cheese, leather and sheep market along with various stalls selling vegetables and other produce.

By the time Becky and her friends arrived into town the cattle market was bustling with the sights and sounds of animals, carts and people. Samuel Haynes lost no time organising his family and assigning them their tasks.

David was to take the rams over to the sheep market and register them with the auctioneer while Mr Haynes made his way to the stalls in the cattle market to see about buying another cow for the milk herd. It was Amy's turn to manage the stall of leeks and cabbages as Mrs Haynes was going to the cheese market.

Banbury hosted a fine cheese market and people travelled from all around to buy the various cheeses that were sold there. Since her husband had started a dairy herd, Mrs Haynes had been experimenting at home with different cheeses. Her aim had been to create a mild and creamy cheddar. Contented, at last, with her efforts she had decided to bring some of her cheese to the market, to try and sell it.

After giving Amy instructions about how much to charge for the vegetables a very nervous Mary Haynes took in a deep breath of air, picked up her basket of cheese and tentatively made her way over to the cheese market.

Normally Amy and Becky would wander around the markets chatting to people they knew and admiring all the animals but today Amy had to work. The two young girls set up their stall and then made themselves comfortable as they waited for customers. While waiting they talked and giggled together.

One of the first people to stop at their stall and buy something was Elizabeth Hardy with little Isabelle holding her hand. Becky held out her arms and Isabelle ran around the stall to give her a hug.

31

"Well I'm surprised to see you two looking so *alert* this morning," commented Mrs Hardy. "I don't expect that you *slept* much in that barn all night!"

"No, not much actually," admitted Becky. "We will probably be tired later."

"Well, thank you for all your help with Isabelle yesterday. All Ron and I heard last night was, 'Becky this' and 'Becky that.'"

"Oh, I enjoyed it," said Becky, bouncing the little girl up and down on her knee. "We had fun."

"Good. I'm glad to hear it," said Mrs Hardy, turning to look at Amy. "Now I need four leeks, two cabbages and we'll fill this can here with some milk please."

Amy gathered the vegetables together and carefully poured some milk from the huge churn into the little metal can that Mrs Hardy had brought along with her. After the girls had sold her vegetables and they had all said goodbye, Amy turned to Becky and pulled a face. "I do find Mrs Hardy scary. She's always so stern and strict."

"Yes I know what you mean," replied Becky, "but I don't think that she means it."

As the morning went by many different people stopped to buy things and the girls were really enjoying themselves. Just after noon David came to join them. The two rams had sold for a good price and he was pleased with himself. As the three of them were sat eating cheese and chutney sandwiches Mr Webb approached the stall.

George Webb was one of the town's policemen. He had grown up with Aunt Rosa and so knew Becky quite well. When Becky was younger she remembered him being a jolly, light-hearted man but three years ago he joined the police force and it seemed that he had left his sense of humour with his previous job.

"Working today are you Rebecca?" he asked sharply.

"No Sir," she replied. "I'm just spending the day with my friend."

George Webb's beady little eyes turn their attention to Amy. "You working?"

Amy wasn't quite as polite or helpful as her friend had been. This wasn't the first time that she had been questioned by Constable Webb about the amount of time she spent *working* on the farm. Knowing that he struggled with his hearing in busy, noisy environments, she looked down at the cabbages and mumbled in a low tone. "I don't work for money. I'm helping Father out and I like it."

"What's that?" retorted the policeman, beginning to go red in the face. "Speak up child!"

David stood up and addressed him, "Look Mr Webb, Sir. You know our family. Amy doesn't *work*, as you put it, but very occasionally she helps when we are busy. Father and Mother run the farm, I'll be sixteen next month and taking on a lot more responsibility then. Now would you like to buy something, Sir?"

"No I do not want to buy anything. Where is your father?" he demanded.

"Father is over by the cattle, Sir," David replied and George Webb marched off. Amy sat down indignantly. "Why won't he leave us alone?!" she snapped.

"Well he has got to enforce the law," explained David. "Also Amy, you need to be careful how you speak to him. He is a policeman after all."

"What's the problem? Why is he bothering you?" asked Becky.

"It's the child labour laws," started David. "The laws are strict now about the amount of time young children can work each day, which is great. It means that poor young kids can't carry on slaving for hours and hours in the factories but it also means that some police officers like to try and find fault with farmers. Especially those like George Webb who struggle to pin anything on the factories and so for the sake of something to do, look elsewhere to pass the time. Amy likes to help out on the farm. We know it's not intense labour but others don't want to see it that way."

"It really annoys me! He doesn't pick on the Hawkins or the Savages like he picks on us," grumbled Amy.

"Well that's probably got something to do with Father. You know George Webb used to be quite sweet on our mother and well...it's obvious who was the better man and ended up winning that battle!"

The girl's mouths dropped to the ground at this revelation and David quickly changed the subject.

"I tell you what," said David. "I'll watch the stall now. Why don't you two go and have a wander about."

Becky and Amy set off in the direction of the cheese market, giggling together at the thought of stuffy police Officer Webb flirting with Amy's mother. Along the way they admired some of the calves that were for sale in the cattle market. Amy particularly liked a small brown bullock that had long black eyelashes. She leaned through the fence and blew warm air onto his face and then laughed out loud as he licked his nose with his long, wet tongue.

As they passed by the horses, Becky saw a few people that she recognised from the canal and they nodded to her by way of a greeting.

When they reached the cheese market the girls looked around, hunting for Mary Haynes. They were finding it difficult to see her and then Amy noticed that there was one stall that appeared to be rather popular. Quite a few people were standing by it. As Amy looked beyond the small crowd to behind the stall she could see her mother's beaming smile. Tugging Becky's arm and pointing excitedly at the stall she said, "Look! There she is! Over there. Where all those people are!"

They made their way over to the stall and wriggled between chattering housewives to get to the front. Amy looked at the table and then stared, open-mouthed at her mother. "It's....it's all gone!" she exclaimed in disbelief.

Mary Haynes' cheese was a success. Almost everyone

who had tried it had liked it and had bought some.

Mrs Haynes smiled at her daughter and nodded her head happily.   She then continued with her conversation. The sale of Mary Haynes' new cheese had prompted many to ask why she had started making it.   This had led to a discussion about the declining wool trade. Many of the farmer's families were in the same situation and the wives were now busy debating the advantages and disadvantages of their husband's new business ideas.   Realising that they weren't going to get much attention while this discussion was in full flow, Becky and Amy wriggled their way out through the group of women, and meandered back towards the vegetables.

Reaching the cattle market they stopped for a second time. As they were standing again with their heads through the fence making noises at the calves a voice called out from behind them.

"Well if it isn't my little Rebecca and her mischievous friend, Amy."

"Aunt Rosa!" Becky quickly pulled her head out from the fence and turned to look at her aunty. There she was, small and plump with flushed pink cheeks standing behind a small barrow full of all kinds of food.

"I was wondering if we would see you!" She ran over and gave Aunt Rosa a big hug.

"Well I'm glad I bumped into you," she replied.   "I wanted to tell you to come and see me tomorrow. Oh, and bring a basket. Mr and Mrs Hamilton are holding a private dinner party tonight. Now, I can't stop. Bye!"

"Okay, I'll see you tomorrow," Becky waved her goodbye.

"What was that all about?" asked Amy.

"Well, whenever Mrs Hamilton has one of her dinner parties up at the Coaching Inn there is always heaps of food left over. They probably drink so much that they forget to eat. Anyway, good old Aunt Rosa always saves me some of the leftovers."

They were now back at the stall. David was packing up what was left of the vegetables and Mr Haynes was tying a big, black and white Friesian to the cart to take home and join his small herd.

"Come on then you two," he called to David and Amy when everything was loaded and ready to go. "We'll go over to the cheese market and get your mother. Take care Becky. See you soon I expect. Oh, and thank you for all your help today."

Amy hugged her friend and then jumped up onto the back of the vegetable cart. Becky waved them all goodbye. Then she turned and set off towards the canal and the little lockhouse.

5

Approaching the lock, still excited about the events of the previous two days, Becky could see her father chopping wood over by the house. Carefully walking across the narrow, wooden gate of the lock she called out to him. He briefly looked up and then nodded to her as he turned his attention back to the pile of logs. Eager to tell her father about all the things that she had done, Becky perched on a large rock that lay by the front door and waited patiently for him to finish what he was doing.

Splitting the last log in two, Jim Bailey stood the axe up against the doorway, wiped the back of his hand across his sweaty forehead and turned to face his daughter. He was puffing slightly from the exertion of heaving the heavy axe over his head many times.

"Did Mr Hardy give you bread and the pie?" asked Becky.

"Yes. He did. I quite like Mary Haynes' pies." He turned back around and started to stack the logs into a small lean-to that was under the window.

Becky remained quietly sat on the rock twisting her fingers together. She was desperate to tell him everything that she had done but she knew better than to interrupt her father when he was busy.

Jim Bailey continued stacking the logs neatly, one on top of the other, uncomfortably aware that his daughter was still sitting behind him. It made him uneasy when she 'hovered' around like this. It usually meant that she was in a lively mood and he felt awkward with her buoyant conversations.

Reluctantly, and without looking at her, he asked, "Did you have a nice time?"

"Yes," Becky replied. She paused....and then continued a little hesitantly. "Isabelle loved the journey to Aynho."

The back of Jim Bailey's head nodded once to acknowledge her statement.

"She was quite scared of the swing bridge."

Becky nervously watched as her father's head nodded once again. It seemed as though he was actually, really listening to her. Becky relaxed a little, smoothed out the hem of her skirt and started to smile.

"Well it was quite funny actually. You see, I went to try and lift the bridge and...."

As Becky told her tales of the activities that had taken place over the last two days she didn't take her eyes off her father. He didn't look at her or ask any questions but neither did he tell her to stop talking. As Becky got further into her story, she gradually became more excited, her voice became louder and her speech more animated as she chattered away about her night in the barn, and her experience milking the cow.

Jim Bailey could sense the feeling of panic increasing with each new sentence that the child began. His wife, Myriam, had used to tell stories in this way. In those days he had enjoyed the sound of her cheerful chatter. He used to find her animated way of speaking enchanting and he would continually ask questions just so that he could keep listening to the sound of her voice. But that was then. Myriam was gone. And this was now. Hearing this excited voice coming from the little girl that was sat behind him, he felt disconnected from her and the vibrant chatter started to scare him. It scared him because it brought back memories that he had tried hard to forget. It scared him because he didn't know how to react to it. So he stayed silent, concentrating on the pile of logs, desperately trying to ignore the emotions that were churning around inside of him.

Just then, as Becky was proudly telling him about her experiences in the milking shed, Fidget came bounding around the corner and suddenly pounced directly onto the troubled man's feet.

Struggling to control the feelings inside and shocked by the kitten's playful attack, Jim Bailey completely over-reacted.

Letting out an unrestrained yell of anger he picked the kitten up and threw it at his daughter.

"Rebecca! I told you to keep that thing out of my way! Now, can't you see that I'm busy?!"

In an instant, Becky's face had turned white and salty wet tears quickly filled her eyes. Biting her lip to stop herself from crying she clutched the small, shaking kitten tightly against her chest, and ran straight into the house.

Furious with himself for losing his temper and pained by the image of his daughter's distraught face, Jim Bailey turned around and with an angry yell of rage he hurled the last few logs onto the pile.

6

The following morning, after Becky and her father had eaten breakfast in a subdued silence and she had cleared away the dishes and tidied up the kitchen, she took Fidget out into the garden and spent some time playing with him. She had spent most of the night sobbing into her pillow and even the fresh spring air and the bounces of the energetic kitten couldn't lighten her dejected mood. Mid-morning she reluctantly set off to visit her Aunt Rosa, carrying with her an empty basket as instructed.

It was a misty day and Becky made her way across the lock and down the side of the great big corn mill to get to the road. The corn mill was one of the town's busiest factories and the road outside was always full of horses and carts making deliveries to and from the gigantic building. The young girl squeezed her way between the carts and workers and then passed the big town hall as she continued up Parsons Street towards North Bar. As she walked along the narrow street Becky greeted Mrs Pennycad who was sweeping the steps outside the Olde Reindeer Inn. Mr Pennycad was the landlord there. Besides the fact that Tom Watkins, Becky's uncle, spent a lot of time drinking there, Mrs Pennycad was a very good friend of Aunt Rosa's. Mrs Pennycad called out to Becky to give her regards to her Aunt Rosa and Becky assured her that she would.

At the top of Parsons Street Becky turned left and passed by St Mary's Church, looking somewhat eerie surrounded by wisps of white foggy cloud. She felt very small next to the magnificent building. Pausing opposite the Whately Coaching Inn, Becky looked down the road through the misty haze towards the cross. She wasn't the only one who was taking in this view. A few others had stopped to look at the impressive new monument. As a horse and cart passed alongside the cross, a little boy was sat up front next to his father; he tugged at the older man's shirt and pointed up at the stone structure.

Centuries ago the sight of a cross in Banbury was not something unusual. The town used to be home to three crosses; the Bread cross, the High cross and the White cross. However, many decades before, the town council had the three crosses destroyed. For over two hundred years the children of Banbury had grown up singing a rhyme about a cross that they had never seen. But now that tuneful little rhyme had meaning. To commemorate the marriage of Princess Victoria, this new cross had been erected during the previous year and was rapidly becoming a focal point for the town. As Becky crossed over the road she started humming the well-known little rhyme to herself and it started to lift her melancholy spirits.

When Becky reached the Whately Coaching Inn she walked round to the stables in the main yard. Both her Uncle Tom and Cousin Joshua worked in the yard. Aunt Rosa and Uncle Tom had both worked at the inn from their early teens and continued on as staff after they had married. Uncle Tom's job was to clean and repair the coaches and carriages as they came through the inn as well as to drive Mr and Mrs Hamilton's carriages whenever they went anywhere. Joshua worked as a stable hand. Entering the yard, Becky could see Joshua wiping down a beautiful black mare. He waved to her and she went over to say hello. Becky liked her cousin Joshua but being almost three years younger she always felt like a nuisance to him. He was fifteen years old, the same age as David, but not nearly as jolly. Quiet and sullen, he worked hard and didn't say much. He certainly didn't take after his mother, Aunt Rosa, who was well known in the town for her high spirits.

"Hello Josh," said Becky, stroking the soft velvety nose of the big black horse. "I've come to have tea break with Aunt Rosa.

"Yes, Mother mentioned you were coming. Father's already inside. I'll be there in a minute. I've just got to give this one some water." He led the horse into one of the stables and Becky made her way over to the kitchen door, which was in the corner of the yard.

"Ah Becky. There you are," said Aunt Rosa, all flushed from peeling potatoes.

Aunt Rosa was the head cook for the entire inn, including the personal meals for Mr Hamilton and his wife. Each day there were meals to prepare for the guests along with the many other people who stopped by this central meeting point. As well as the paying guests, the Hamiltons frequently entertained their personal friends and Aunt Rosa also had to oversee these occasions. She had been well promoted since the time her and her sister Myriam had worked as young maids. Thankfully Aunt Rosa didn't work alone, there were many girls that helped in the kitchen and Becky noticed one of them leave the large kitchen to take her tea break in the servant's parlour.

"Have a seat dear. The kettle's nearly boiled."

Hesitantly, Becky went over to the big oak table where her uncle was eating a slice of sponge cake and sat down opposite him. She was rather scared of Uncle Tom. In fact she always wondered how he and her Aunt Rosa had ended up married to each other. Tall with a mass of red hair, he was fierce looking and unpredictable. Sometimes, if he hadn't been drinking, he could be quite nice and polite but when he'd been on the bottle he developed a sharp temper and forgot his manners. Becky had seen this happen once or twice and it frightened her. Therefore, she was always on her guard whenever he was around. Today though, he seemed to be in a good mood so Becky relaxed.

"What's all this I hear about a kitten?" he asked, passing her a piece of the cake.

Becky looked up at him. "Oh. You mean Fidget. Well my friend Amy gave him to me as a gift. But Uncle Tom....how did you know? I've only just got him recently?"

"I popped over to see your father yesterday morning," he replied. "He's a likeable little fella, that kitten, I must say. Although, I don't think your father would agree. He didn't look too keen on the little thing if you ask me."

"No," admitted Becky, letting out a little sigh, "but

then I don't think there's much that Father is keen on."

"And that's me included," added Uncle Tom. "We've never really seen eye to eye on matters. I didn't hang around too long yesterday...didn't feel too welcome."

Aunt Rosa looked up from where she was standing across the kitchen. She had sensed that the child was in low spirits. "How is your father these days, my duckie?" she asked with a look of concern on her face.

"Oh. Okay. Well you know," replied Becky, biting her lip as she remembered the outburst that had taken place on the previous evening.

At that moment Joshua came into the kitchen and Aunt Rosa quickly changed the conversation to tales of the dinner party that had taken place the night before. Becky began to look less troubled and soon started to smile. She asked all about the ladies' dresses and Aunt Rosa described it all in great detail for her. When they had finished their tea and cake Uncle Tom and Joshua went back out into the yard to continue working while Becky and Aunt Rosa remained sat at the table.

"Time is a great healer," commented Aunt Rosa.

Becky looked up at her, slightly confused by what she had said.

Aunt Rosa continued, "We all miss your mother very much. Some of us cope better than others. But, as I said, time is a great healer. In time your father will heal and then he'll realize that he's got the next best thing to your mother right in front of him. So you just hang in there and don't forget that you can have a great big cuddle from your Aunt Rosa any time you want."

The big round lady held the little skinny girl tight and Becky felt a warm feeling come over her.

"However," continued Aunt Rosa, "I need to get on with the cooking or the paying customers upstairs won't get their lunch. Here you are, I've put a few goodies together from last night. Pop them in your basket there. That should cheer your father up a little anyway."

"Thank you," said Becky as the kitchen girls arrived back in the room to continue working. She gave Aunt Rosa a quick kiss on the cheek then made her way back home feeling a little happier than when she had set out that morning.

7

The next few weeks passed by much as any others and life on the canal was as pleasant as any for those who worked and lived there. However, one Monday at the end of April the rain clouds came over and darkened not only the sky above Oxfordshire but also the livelihood of many families living there.

Betty, who came each week to wash Jim and Rebecca Bailey's clothes, had just finished and Becky had made her a cup of tea. Sipping on the hot tea Betty commented about the dark clouds that were gathering overhead.

"If I were you Becky, I would get the fire going and hang those clothes indoors."

"Yes. I think I will," replied Becky. "It looks like this could be more than a shower."

Just as she finished talking the first drops of rain began to fall, making circular ripples on the surface of the canal as they hit the water.

"I'm going to make a dash for home before this gets worse," said Betty, standing up to go. "Thank you for the tea. Tell your father I'll collect my wages later."

Betty ran off up the tow path towards the stables where she and her husband lived.

As the raindrops became heavier and increased in number Becky quickly gathered up the clothes and teacups and ran indoors. She lit the fire and hung the clothes up on a line above the fireplace then sunk down into an armchair and stared out of the window.

The raindrops were now falling as a steady downpour. Becky could see that her father had put on his overcoat and was sat on the opposite side of the canal with Mr Dickenson in his coal shed taking shelter. A few people were running along the tow path, hurriedly making their way home, away from the rain.

Becky was still staring out of the window when she heard a faint 'meow'. Jumping up and running to open the door she called out, "Hold on Fidget. I'm coming."

She threw open the door and in crept the dripping wet kitten looking very sorry for himself. Finding an old towel, Becky rubbed Fidget dry and he lay out in front of the roaring fire to warm up. Looking out the window again Becky could see her father sending a barge through the lock. He had his head bowed low against the rain.

She spent the afternoon sat in the armchair drawing in her sketchbook and cuddling Fidget. Every now and then she would look out of the window at the rain and let out a sigh. Becky spent most of her life outdoors and she was getting restless being shut up inside all day. Looking out as the day passed and watching her father battling with the rain she decided that he probably was not in the best of moods either. Dreading the thought of him coming in from work short-tempered Becky packed up her sketchbook and went through to the kitchen to light the stove and cook him a tasty hot meal.

When it was dark and movement on the canal had slowed to a halt, Jim Bailey came into the house. Becky could hear him grumbling to himself while he stood in the hallway taking off his wet clothes. She quickly shooed the kitten away from the fireplace and placed a plate of hot mashed potato and sausages beside her father's armchair.

Jim Bailey came into the room looking worn-out and fed up. Becky noticed his eyes light up a little when he saw the steaming plate of hot food and they sat together in front of the fire to eat. He was enjoying his meal so much that he didn't notice the black and white kitten crawl back into the room and lay in front of the fireplace.

After he finished his last mouthful Jim Bailey wiped his lips, put his plate down on the floor and looked across the room at his daughter.

"Thank you Rebecca. That was just what I needed."

He rarely thanked her for anything so Becky knew that she had done well. Watching her father settle down into his armchair she took the opportunity to start a conversation.

"The puddles look as though they are getting deep out there."

"Yes," he replied. "Poor Bob has got a few leaks in the shed roof so I helped him to move some of the coal earlier."

"Oh dear. Poor Mr Dickenson," said Becky. "I'm sorry that all the washing is everywhere, but I needed somewhere to hang it to dry."

Sensing that the child wanted to make this into a conversation Jim Bailey laid his head back against the cushion of the chair. "I'm tired from moving all that coal. Why don't you take that cat of yours out to the kitchen and teach it to hunt while I rest a bit."

Becky opened her mouth to reply but he had already closed his eyes so she picked Fidget up and left the room.

The rain didn't stop all night and when Becky woke up the next morning she could still see the trickles of rain running down the outside of her window. She got up out of bed to look outside at the landscape. Then with a gasp of shock she quickly ran downstairs.

Her father was sitting in the kitchen quietly drinking a cup of hot tea when Becky burst in.

"Father! Have you seen the canal?" she asked.

From her bedroom window, at the front of the house, Becky had seen that the water in the canal was unusually high. It was in fact barely an inch away from the bank. She had never seen the water so high before.

"It's okay," he replied. "There are hundreds of overflow points. Besides, I've been out and taken some level readings. Yes the canal is high, but as I said, it's built to cope with extra water. Now call me when breakfast is ready. I want to check on Bob."

51

About an hour later, when they had finished breakfast, Becky put on her overcoat and boots and went out into the rain. She walked along the tow path curious to see the overflow points that her father had mentioned.

Mr Bailey knew what he was talking about. Part of his job as lock keeper was to take regular readings along the canal, also checking these overflow points and to pass this information back to the canal authorities. The canals were handmade and so contained no natural water flow like that of a river. This meant that, as well as needing extra water at times, there potentially was nowhere for any excess water to go. So as the men had dug out the canals as well as including water source points, they had also built overflow points so that extra water had somewhere to flow away to. Becky's father was right. Along the canal there were many of these points and Becky could see water rushing through them. Most of them ran out into little streams that joined the River Cherwell which ran alongside the canal. Normally the River Cherwell was nothing more than a trickling brook but today it was a violently rushing river. As Becky stood there in the pouring rain she could see that the river was almost bursting its banks. Heading back along the tow path, Becky returned home to dry off.

Every few hours, Mr Bailey made his checks along the tow path and the canal seemed to be coping just as it had been designed to, but he couldn't help noticing how high the water in the nearby river was getting and it made him feel a little uncomfortable. The rain continued all that day and through a second night. Then, early Wednesday morning it became horribly obvious that something was wrong. When Jim Bailey awoke the relentless rain had turned to a light drizzle and although everyone was preparing themselves for the day's work ahead, the movement of traffic on the canal was non-existent. Not a single barge had come through the lock since dawn almost two hours ago. Jim Bailey was not good at standing idle and he was soon pacing up and down, alongside the lock, muttering to himself. He couldn't understand why no barges were moving through. Especially as mid-week was usually his busiest time.

Then, just as Becky was getting dressed in her bedroom, Ben came running down from Mr Hardy's timber yard.

"Mr Bailey. Sir! Mr Dickenson!" he gasped, breathing heavily.

Both men approached the boy with a questioning look on their faces.

"It's the river, Sir," Ben explained. "It's flooded. The river's flooded!"

"What do you mean boy?" asked Mr Dickenson.

"Well the early morning delivery hadn't arrived, so Mr Hardy sent me out to walk north and see what was going on. It's flooded. The River Cherwell has broken its bank. I had to walk a good mile but it's true. All the water is in the canal. The canal is flooded too!"

By this time Becky had come downstairs and looked out of the kitchen window, which faced the back of the house. With a scream she ran to the front and swung the door open.

"Father! The garden is flooded down the bottom. I can't see the vegetable patch at all! Quick we have to save the hens!"

"Silence a minute Rebecca! There are bigger problems out here."

Jim Bailey looked back at Ben in confused disbelief. "Are you sure about the canal? I mean it sounds like the river has flooded my garden but the canal here is okay."

"I don't know how to explain it Sir," Ben replied. "The ground undulates all the time. All I know is what I saw with my own eyes, and I saw the river and canal as one!"

Jim Bailey turned to Mr Dickenson. "I'm just going to walk south along the tow path and see what's happening."

He had not walked more than five hundred yards around the corner before he could see that the canal south of the lock had flooded too. Here the river and the canal were separated by the railway but the river water had risen above the tracks making them invisible. The wonderfully designed overflow points were now submerged in a great sea of water. It was as if they didn't exist. The canal and the river were running as one body of water with the tow path lying somewhere beneath. There was no way anything could travel along the canal as no one could tell where its banks began or ended.

For the town this was a disaster. The canal was the main transport route for goods between the Midlands and London. Companies situated further away from the canal used coaches or carts but for the few that had begun to use the railway there was no movement either. The flooding had affected the majority of the town's industries because of a lack of vital transportation.

It took three days for the flood water to subside. Many homes and factories had flooded and many barges had been damaged. Almost everyone who worked on the canal received no wage and during those three days the town lost a lot of money. Spirits were low and tempers were short.

When the rain stopped later that day and for a few days after, Becky stayed as far from the lockhouse as she possibly could. When she was at home she stayed quiet and kept herself and Fidget out of her father's way. Jim Bailey spent those three days walking around with a thunder cloud over his head. His temper was like a lightning bolt waiting to strike at anything or anyone that provoked him.

Thankfully by Saturday afternoon the waters had subsided enough for a few barges to move along the canal. Many who had become restless while waiting for the canal to re-open were able to start working again and spirits started to rise.

8

The following Monday was 'Mayday' and it came at just the right time to cheer up the inhabitants of Banbury town.

Becky got up early to collect the eggs and make breakfast for her father. While they sat eating she broke the silence to remind him that it was Mayday.

"So," he replied. "Of what interest is it to me?"

"Well," answered Becky. "Most of the townsfolk will be at the celebrations. I thought that maybe we could go together."

She didn't look at her father. Instead she fixed her eyes down at her plate of breakfast. This was a day for families to be out together and Becky desperately wanted him to go along with her.

"Rebecca! You may not realize but two weeks ago I lost three days good wages. I'll be damned if I'm foolish enough to give up a fourth day's earnings just to watch people skipping around a maypole whilst I idly stand around watching."

As he was talking a thought crossed her mind and she looked up at him.

"But Father," she said hesitantly. "Most of the businesses will be closed. I doubt there will be anyone on the canal today."

Irritated by his daughter's inability to reason beyond the childish fun and games of a maypole dance, Jim Bailey pushed his plate into the middle of the table, slid his chair back and abruptly stood up.

"I'm not the only man concerned about making a living. There will be people on this canal and I will be waiting here to work the lock for them. One day you'll realize that there's more to life than fun and games!"

With that he pulled his cap firmly onto his head and left the kitchen.

Bitterly disappointed, Becky felt a small lump start to choke her throat. But then she remembered that today was Mayday and that she wanted to enjoy it. So, after blinking her eyes and gulping down a glass of water she quickly cleared away the breakfast things and got ready to go. She put on her favourite dress. It was pink and white with a laced hem. She brushed her hair out and tied a pink ribbon into the back, and then popped her best white bonnet on top.

As Becky approached the town hall she could see that much of the road had been fenced off to stop carts and carriages from coming through. The town was busy and there were people milling around everywhere. In front of the town hall was a tall maypole with beautiful ribbons of all different colours hanging down from the top. Next to the maypole was a small silver band playing an array of different folk songs. On the steps of the town hall Becky could see many people walking up and down, going in and out. Feeling happier surrounded by all this merriment, Becky lifted her chin up a little and set off towards the town hall.

Inside there were many stalls selling all kinds of crafts and foods. Casually wandering around Becky stopped now and then to look at hats, jewellery and various other handmade items. After twenty minutes or so she bumped into her Aunt Rosa.

"There you are my dear. I've been looking for you everywhere," she held Becky tight and the young girl felt her mouth twitch and turn upwards into a beaming smile. Then, holding Becky out at arm's length to look at her, Aunt Rosa frowned and her eyes searched about behind Becky.

"Well, where's your father? Have you lost him already?"

Becky's smile dropped. "No. He didn't come," she replied. "He says we lost too much money last week."

Knowing her brother-in-law's anti-social ways Aunt Rosa nodded to herself.

"Oh well. I've lost Tom to Mr Pennycad's drinking house and young Joshua didn't want to walk around with his 'mam.' So it looks as though we'll have to keep each other company. Now, young Miss Bailey, it looks to me like you need a good old Banbury cake."

They went over to a stall where Mr Brown, the baker, was selling his cakes. While Becky tucked into the delicious, fruit filled, sugary pastry she and Aunt Rosa made their way back outside to where the band was playing. They spotted Mr and Mrs Hardy standing down by the maypole and so they went over to say hello. Ron Hardy explained to them that he had closed the timber yard for the day to join in the celebrations and Becky hurriedly pushed away thought of her father back at the lockhouse.

"Where's Isabelle?" she asked, looking around the area where they were standing.

"Over there," replied Mrs Hardy, pointing to the maypole.

One of the dancers was teaching some of the very small children how to skip around the pole whilst holding the brightly coloured ribbon in their hands. Not really concentrating, little Isabelle was jumping about in a circle while waving and blowing kisses to her mother and father.

"She is growing up Elizabeth," said Aunt Rosa. "With those big brown eyes, she looks just like Ron."

"I know," replied Mrs Hardy. "She's a proper little girl now, not a baby anymore."

Laughing at the small child jumping around, Becky noticed a hand waving at her from across the other side of the maypole. Looking closely she could see that it was Amy. Aunt Rosa had also seen her.

"Well if you'd all excuse me, I need to get back to the kitchens. And Becky, I think that someone over on the other side is trying to get your attention."

Becky grinned at her aunty. "Yes. I think so. Thank you for the cake. Goodbye Mr and Mrs Hardy." Becky hugged Aunt Rosa and then ran off to join Amy.

"Such a sweet girl," commented Mr Hardy.

"Yes," agreed Aunt Rosa. "She's becoming more and more like her mother each day."

The three adults nodded thoughtfully for a moment and then Aunt Rosa made her way home passing by the Olde Reindeer but not stopping by to see what her husband was up to.

9

After wandering around for a couple of hours, Becky and Amy sat on the steps that led up to the town hall exchanging stories about the recent flooding of the river. Becky had to hold on to her belly as she burst into laughter at Amy's vivid description of Mr Haynes and David standing knee deep in dirty river water, trying to pull the cows out of the bottom field. According to Amy, her brother had ended up sat down in the flooded field on more than one occasion.

As they were talking, the area directly around the maypole was cleared and the dancers came out wearing beautiful dresses. The two girls finished their conversation and focused their attention to the scene in front of them. The first of May was one of the biggest holidays of the year and the maypole dance was the highlight of this day. All over the country, in every village, town and city there were young ladies dancing in their best dresses around a maypole on Mayday.

The dancers spread out equally around the maypole, each facing different directions, and each holding one of the brightly coloured ribbons in their hands. There was a hushed, anticipated silence for a few moments from the crowd of spectators around the maypole. Then on the count of four the band started to play a lively folk tune and the dancers began to skip delicately around the pole. While dancing, they

61

skilfully weaved in and out as they passed by one another. Eagerly watching while the tune and the dancing continued, the two girls could see that descending from the top of the maypole a spectacular pattern of colour was being woven around and down the trunk of the pole. The individual colours were masterfully knitted together as the dancers crossed in and out and were gently pulled closer to the centre as the ribbons in their hands gradually wrapped around and around. The dancers then repeated this graceful routine in reverse until all the ribbons were again hanging freely.

While Amy enjoyed watching the dancing, she did find the whole process a little time consuming and soon started to look about to see who was sitting nearby. Becky however, was fascinated by the decorative scene that was in front of her. Her gaze was transfixed and she couldn't take her eyes off the brightly coloured maypole surrounded by elegant dancers. Because her mother had died when Becky was young and her father never went out to social events, she had not seen a great deal of folk dancing like this. Becky herself had never learned to dance. As she sat watching, she desperately wished that someone would teach her so that she could one day dance like this and wear such a beautiful dress.

When the music came to an end and the dancers finished, the crowd enthusiastically applauded. Becky stood up and clapped her hands together as hard as she could. The dancers then scurried off to change their clothes and the crowd started to move away. Becky and Amy linked arms and began to skip around the maypole singing a popular little tune to themselves. While they were still jumping about David, Mr Haynes and a few other men suddenly came running towards them and then headed up towards Parsons Street.

"Hey! What's wrong?" called Amy as her brother carried on past where they were standing.

"Your cousin Josh needs some help Becky. I think that Uncle of yours has got himself into a bit of trouble," David called out, not stopping. "They're in the Olde Reindeer."

Becky looked at Amy and raised her eyebrows. "I expect he's been drinking all day and now he's fighting. Poor Aunt Rosa, she really doesn't deserve such a fierce husband."

Becky's estimation was correct. Tom Watkins had spent most of the day inside the inn drinking away his wages from the previous week. With the canals out of action he had earned more than usual driving the coaches and hence had been drinking more than usual too.

Tom and his fellow drinkers had started the day with simple games of dominoes and cards. However, with the passing of time and alcohol they moved on to arm wrestling and then actual wrestling. The Mayday celebrations had brought two types of people together into one another's company. Townsfolk who were used to drinking with each other were now joined by the farmers and country men who had brought their families into town for the day. The mixture or alcohol and pride meant that many of the men did not want to be humiliated in front of friends and fellow workmates and so many resorted to cheating.

Although not a large man, Tom Watkins worked with horses and so was deceptively strong. Later on in the afternoon, after the wrestling had begun, he came up against a big, thick set farmer who had travelled in from the nearby hamlet of Neithrop. Starting to lose to Tom but not wanting to look a fool in front of a group of his companions that had been stood watching, the hefty farmer played a couple of dirty moves. With the anger beginning to boil inside, Tom Watkins wrestled harder still and his opponent continued to slip back more and more. Afraid to lose and spurred on by arrogance, the young farmer threw a sneaky punch that split the flesh on Tom Watkins left cheekbone. With his senses dulled by the alcohol his aggression turned to fury and he was instantly at the farmer's throat, threatening to kill him.

By the time David and the others arrived outside, the Olde Reindeer was the centre of a small riot. Samuel Haynes, his son and the others couldn't even get close to the doorway to go in and drag Tom Watkins out.

As half a dozen police officers ran past the maypole, and on up to Parsons Street, blowing their whistles, Amy asked Becky if she wanted to go and see what was happening.

"No, thank you," replied Becky. "There will be a group of men bruised and bleeding. The police will take the instigators, probably Uncle Tom included, away for the night while everyone else clears up the broken chairs and smashed glass. I've seen it before Amy. I'm going to go home. Anyway, Father will be getting hungry."

"But what about your Aunt Rosa?" asked Amy.

"Mrs Pennycad would have left the inn as soon as the trouble started. She'll be in the kitchens at the Whately with Aunt Rosa now."

Amy nodded. "Yes. Poor Aunt Rosa. Well if you're going home I'm going to go and find Mother. See you Becky."

"Yes. See you soon."

The two girls gave each other a hug and headed off in separate directions, away from the sounds of people shouting and police officers blowing their whistles.

Up in the kitchens of the Whately Coaching Inn, Maria Pennycad was comforting her good friend, Rosa Watkins, as she lamented over her husband's foolish behaviour.

ONE FINE LADY

Summer

1

As the weeks passed by and the hours of daylight lengthened, Becky spent more and more time out of doors. Fidget kept increasing in size and Becky sewed a toy mouse out of an old sock in an attempt at training him to hunt. Much to Jim Bailey's annoyance and displeasure however, it seemed that the growing kitten preferred pouncing on his busy, agitated feet to stalking rodents and on more than one occasion the poor little cat had been on the receiving end of the big man's angry swinging right foot. Upset and frustrated, Becky tried her best to keep Fidget out of her father's way but for some unknown reason the small, black and white creature insisted on trying to make friends with the grumpy, short-tempered man.

This is exactly the way things went one morning when Aunt Rosa popped by. She had some leftover slices of ham from the night before and brought them down to the lockhouse for Becky and her father. Becky was out, up at Ron Hardy's yard playing with Isabelle. Jim Bailey was in the kitchen making himself a cup of tea. Aunt Rosa called out a cheery hello and made her way inside. She helped herself to a cup and sat down to drink the hot tea.

"Are you busy today?" she asked her brother-in-law. She hated this superficial 'chit-chat' but he was never one for starting a conversation.

"Not bad," he replied.

"Umm," she continued, "there have been a lot of people passing by the inn. Our Josh is flat out in the yard."

Jim Bailey continued slurping at his tea.

"Tom is taking the coach to Oxford today. Mr Hamilton has got a meeting over there or something like that."

"Ah," said Jim Bailey looking up at her. "How is Tom?"

Although Tom Watkins and Jim Bailey both shared a quick temper, the latter held no respect for his sister-in-law's husband. Jim Bailey lost his temper because he carried around a great sadness and sense of loss from when his dear Myriam had died. It made him somehow excuse his actions. However, in his opinion, Tom Watkins deserved no such sympathy for the way he behaved. He drank his wages away in the public houses and then lashed out at the first person who seemed to give a look at him in the wrong way.

Aunt Rosa was well aware of Jim Bailey's feelings towards her husband and so she answered him accordingly.

"Tom is fine, thank you Jim. He has had no more bother with the police, if that's what you're getting at."

"And the cut on his face...it's cleared up has it?"

"It certainly has. He's as handsome as ever." Aunt Rosa kept the tone light. She most definitely didn't intend to allow Jim Bailey to slip into speaking badly

69

of her husband.

He continued, "But really Rosa, what is the man thinking of; getting into fights at his age? It's a shambles. It's what I'd expect of a lad like young Joshua, not of a grown man of Tom's age with responsibilities. I'm sure the Hamiltons couldn't have been impressed over the whole affair."

Feeling annoyed, embarrassed and not wanting to argue with her brother-in-law Aunt Rosa put on her biggest smile possible and stood up to go.

"Well Jim. Thank you for the cup of tea but I must get back to prepare lunch now. I'll just pop that ham in the larder for you."

As she took the ham out from her basket and carried it over to the larder Fidget came out from under the window, where he had been sleeping, to investigate the interesting smell. Once the larder door was shut and the smell of the ham gone he looked around for something else to do and leaped straight onto Jim Bailey's feet.

The man let out a furious yell and grabbed Fidget by the scruff of his neck.

"When will you learn not to do that!" he shouted at the bewildered cat. Jim Bailey then turned and threw the helpless creature out of the back door to land heavily amongst the chickens.

Aunt Rosa's smile dropped and her cheeks flushed redder than ever. Watching what had just happened proved to be too much. She opened her mouth and clearly spoke her mind.

"Jim Bailey! You have the nerve to criticise my husband for losing his temper. You are just as bad. What a hypocrite! At least my Tom picks his battles with men of his own size and not with his daughter's poor, innocent little cat. You should be ashamed, treating a small animal like that!"

Picking up her basket she turned and stormed out of the house leaving her brother-in-law dumbfounded by the outburst.

2

During the warm summer months Becky loved to spend as much time as possible on the farm with Amy. Together they would help to feed the animals, pick the vegetables and, of course, milk the cows. Milking the cows was Becky's favourite part of the farm life and she was getting quite fast at it. She was also learning how to make butter and cheese and Mrs Haynes enjoyed teaching her.

One sunny morning in early June, Becky made her way across the fields towards the Hayneses' farm. As she climbed over the gate into the yard she could she Mr Webb on the other side of the farm walking down the lane, away from the farmhouse, towards the road that led to Banbury. He was wearing his uniform and Becky concluded that this hadn't been a social visit to her friend's family. While Becky was still perched on top of the gate the back door to the farmhouse swung open and Amy came rushing out. Her eyes red from crying, she didn't notice that her friend was sitting up on the gate as she ran furiously into the barn pulling the heavy wooden door shut behind her.

Concerned for her friend, Becky jumped down from the gate and walked over to the barn. Before going in she paused and pressed her ear against the door. Coming from inside she could hear heavy sobs. Becky had never known her friend to cry before and she wondered what terrible thing could have happened to upset her so much.

Knocking gently Becky lifted the latch and pulled the door open. It was dark in the barn and as she stepped inside it took a moment or two for her eyes to adjust. However, she didn't need to see to know where her friend was. Coming from over where the few remaining hay bales were stacked Becky could hear Amy's stifled sniffles. As her eyes gradually became accustomed to the light she could make out Amy's figure sitting, hunched over by the far wall.

"Hey," she said walking over and sitting next to her. "What have you done with my best friend?"

With puffy red eyes Amy turned away from the wall and looked at her, confused.

Becky continued, "Well, my friend Amy is so tough that she never cries. So you must be an imposter. Where is she?"

Amy gave a half smile and then turned back to face the wall and started sobbing again.

"Oh Becky. It's that awful Mr Webb. I hate him!"

"Why? What happened?" Becky asked gently.

Amy turned back to look at her. "It's those stupid laws for the child factory labour. He's obsessed with the thing! He came here this morning. He said he was just 'doing the rounds'. Well I was in the shed helping Father with the milking because David is at school today. So anyway, he came in to talk to Father and saw me milking and well....that was it!"

Amy's face started to turn red with indignation. "We all went into the kitchen to talk and he threatened Father with a fine if Father didn't stop making me work long hours. Father tried to explain that I don't work long hours, in fact I don't really work, I only help and that I like it, but he wouldn't listen! He just kept saying that we would end up having to pay a lot of money in fines. I tried to tell him myself that I love helping on the farm but he ignored me and would only speak to Father. He was so rude Becky! He then issued us with an official warning and then left. Father said that for the time being I'm not allowed to help with the farm work. That's when I started crying and ran out of the house."

"But I don't understand," said Becky. "You've been helping on the farm for years. Hundreds of kids help on farms all over the country. Why is Mr Webb worrying about this so much now?"

"I don't know," shrugged Amy. "Father says that this labour law he keeps referring to was made in 1844, that's sixteen years ago, so it's not a new thing. I think he's so bored now that there are two new officers on the police force that he's got nothing better to do with his time than walk around the countryside annoying farmers and their families. That and his history with Mother..."

"Amy Haynes, that is none of your business!"

The girls looked round to face the voice that had interrupted them. As Amy was finishing her last sentence Mrs Haynes had quietly walked into the barn and overheard what her daughter was saying. "And you should know better than to speak about a police officer in that way," she added firmly.

Embarrassed that her mother had heard what she had said about her, Amy looked over to where Mrs Haynes was standing in the doorway, silhouetted by the bright sunlight behind her.

"I'm sorry Mother. I just feel so angry. Did Father really mean what he said, about me not helping on the farm?"

"Just for a week or two, yes," answered Mrs Haynes. "It's just until this all blows over." Noticing that her daughter's fists were still clenched tightly, she continued, "Anyway, Mr Webb certainly won't be coming back today so come along you two, I could do with some help with the cheese. Oh Becky, were you able to bring me some chives?"

"Yes," replied Becky. "I've got a bagful. Betty was very generous."

Delighted with the success of her cheese, Mary Haynes was experimenting with different herbs and seasoning. Betty, who washed the Bailey's clothes, grew a few herbs in pots and was pleased to help out by donating some fresh chives.

Giving her friend a big hug and linking arms with her, Becky started to tell Amy and Mrs Haynes all about how much Fidget was growing as the three of them made their way across the yard to the farmhouse.

3

By the time David arrived back from school, hungry for his lunch, Mrs Haynes and the two girls were on the last stages of the cheese making process. They had boiled up a great big saucepan of milk, while adding lemon juice and buttermilk to make it curdle. Becky and Amy had carefully drained out the whey through a piece of cheesecloth and they were now busy adding the chives to the leftover curds before packing it into circular cheese moulds and placing it in the larder.

David came in and flopped down in the old armchair that sat in front of the large range cooker.

"I don't know what's more tiring," he said, "sitting at a desk doing arithmetic or driving cows up and down from the bottom field."

"Well at least you have the option!" snapped Amy.

"What's got into you? Did you get out on the wrong side of bed?" retorted David.

"David. Stop it," interrupted Mrs Haynes. "Officer Webb came here today and he gave us an official warning about your sister working on the farm."

"Really?!" David looked surprised.

"Yes," continued Mrs Haynes. "So Amy is going to

stop helping out with the jobs."

"But, it's only for a few weeks!" added Amy quickly. "Just until it blows over."

"Well I don't know why you're looking so sad about it," said David. "Two weeks or so to play about and enjoy yourself...It sounds great to me!"

"At least someone's glad about it," sighed Amy and began to set the table for lunch.

When they had all finished lunch, washed up and put the plates away, Becky and Amy went outside to sort the potatoes. The following day was marketing day and Samuel Haynes had a big pile of potatoes that needed sorting out to take with them.

As the girls were finishing with the potatoes, the farrier arrived to fit new shoes on Star, the big cart horse, and on Sparkle, the lively little pony they used to pull the small trap. David was going to watch the farrier to try and learn a bit about how to shoe a horse so he came and asked Amy to help by holding the horses still. Becky carried on sorting out the remaining potatoes. She spent so much of her life around the horses that came up and down the canal that strangely enough she found the potatoes more interesting.

Star, old and experienced, was easy to shoe. Usually she fell asleep and had to be woken up when the farrier wanted her to change legs. Sparkle, on the other hand, was a bit more difficult. The young white pony was fidgety and didn't like to stand still. He also was more interested in the sights and sounds of the farmyard than in the hay net that was placed in front of his nose to try and distract him. While David knelt down next to the farrier to see how to nail the shoes into the horse's hoof, Amy was having a hard time holding Sparkle nice and still for them.

Without warning a sudden gust of wind blew an empty sack across the yard and startled the little pony. Frightened by the unexpected movement Sparkle jumped to the side and kicked his leg out knocking the farrier over onto the ground. As he kicked his leg out with the iron shoe only partly nailed on, the pony's hoof and shoe caught David sharply on the face. Letting out a tremendous cry of pain David fell onto the floor, his hands clinging to his face.

Having heard the painful shriek, Becky came rushing into the yard and gasped in shock as she saw David lying on the floor. Running over she could see a large open cut that was bleeding heavily. Having seen what Elizabeth Hardy had done two years ago when her father trapped his arm between a barge and the lock, Becky leapt into action. Shouting for Mr and Mrs Haynes she grabbed Amy's shawl that was hanging on the wall and pressed it against David's head, holding it firmly against the area that was bleeding. She then called to Amy, who was standing nearby shaking and stunned, and told her to find a doctor. As Amy ran off towards Bodicote to get Doctor Woodhouse, Samuel Haynes carried his son indoors and laid him on his bed and then propped his head up with a pillow while Becky continued putting pressure on the wound. Confused and shocked David kept trying to sit up and talk but the hard blow of the hoof had rendered his speech incoherent so while they waited for the doctor

Becky calmly and quietly told him stories about the many different people she had met on the canal.

Eventually Doctor Woodhouse arrived and Becky went outside to join Amy who was nervously washing the blood off the stone cobbles. Emotionally exhausted Becky's legs could no longer hold her weight and she slumped down against the wall.

Crying for the second time in one day, Amy sat down next to her friend. Becky put her arm around Amy's shoulders.

"He'll be okay. Doctor Woodhouse is here now."

"But Becky, did you see his face?" The skin was all open. I saw his bones inside. And then the blood...it was awful!" Amy put her head into her hands and continued sobbing.

"As I left the room I heard Doctor Woodhouse say that the wound was mainly around the cheek. He told your father that was a good thing," comforted Becky.

"I hope so Becky. I really do."

Mary Haynes made a pot of tea and called the girls inside. A very sensible, level-headed woman, she told Amy to stop crying and started to darn some socks. After about an hour Doctor Woodhouse and Mr Haynes came into the kitchen. Amy jumped up and stared intently at both of them.

"It's okay my duckie. Your brother will live," said Doctor Woodhouse, stroking his long brown beard. "He might not be as good looking as he used to be and he certainly won't be doing much for a week or two but he'll be right as rain before too long. And I must congratulate you young lady," he said, turning to address Becky. "You helped to stop the bleeding and settle his heart rate by talking calmly to him. Well done."

Mary and Samuel Haynes smiled and Amy grinned proudly. Feeling embarrassed and with her cheeks flushed pink, Becky stood up.

"Well it's getting late. I need to get back to Father. I'm glad that David is going to be okay."

"Are you going into Banbury?" asked Doctor Woodhouse.

"Yes. To the lockhouse," she explained.

"Well I need to see a patient in town so I can take you in the trap."

As Becky said goodbye to everyone Mrs Haynes gave her a big hug. "Thank you for all your help today."

Mrs Haynes' comments gave Becky a feeling of warmth and appreciation. Trying to hide an embarrassed, but happy smile, she climbed up onto the trap and sat down next to Doctor Woodhouse. After saying goodbye they set off towards Banbury.

When they reached the canal and Mr Dickenson's coal shed Becky jumped down from the trap and thanked Doctor Woodhouse for the ride home.

"I'll come with you," he said. "I want to congratulate your father on raising such a sensible, quick-thinking daughter."

"Well Father may be busy." She tried in vain to prevent him from following her into the house.

"Nonsense," he insisted. "No father is ever too busy to hear praise for his daughter. Now lead the way."

Feeling uncomfortable and somewhat wary Becky led Doctor Woodhouse past the coal shed and over the lock towards the small cottage. Her father was in the kitchen standing over the stove making a cup of tea. Hearing the front door close he shouted out. "It's about time Rebecca. While you're out laughing and giggling up at that farm, I'm left back here to starve! Don't be forgetting your priorities. I've just about had it with your..."

Jim Bailey, hearing a subtle, unfamiliar cough behind him and turning around to see Doctor Woodhouse standing just behind his daughter in the doorway, stopped mid-sentence.

"Forgive the unannounced intrusion Mr Bailey. I just wanted to quickly congratulate you," explained Doctor Woodhouse.

Annoyed with his daughter for being late and now for bringing this stranger into the house without warning, Jim Bailey raised his eyebrows sharply at Doctor Woodhouse.

Confused by the man's angry expression Doctor Woodhouse continued. "Well, umm, you see, umm. Well the thing is Mr Bailey, your daughter was very brave today and helped a young boy who was very badly hurt."

Becky looked up at her father, smiling nervously.

"Wonderful!" replied Mr Bailey with a harsh tone of sarcasm in his voice. Becky's nervous smile dropped instantly.

"That's absolutely wonderful! She likes to help people. She just forgets to help her *own* father, that's all!"

Giving Becky a sharp glare he turned back to his cup of tea.

Startled and embarrassed by this man's insensitive behaviour Doctor Woodhouse clumsily excused himself. Becky showed him out of the house and then, after taking a deep breath, returned to the kitchen to go and face her father.

As the warm summer sun began to cast shadows across the water Doctor Woodhouse made his way back across the lock. As he walked he shook his head in disbelief and muttered to himself under his breath.

4

One Thursday morning, almost two weeks after David's terrible accident, Becky was making her way across the lock towards town when she heard someone calling her name. She looked up the canal, in the direction of the Hardys' wood yard, to see Ron Hardy jogging towards her with Isabelle on his back. Trying to hold on while her father's legs carried them both up and down the little girl was laughing out loud. Becky could hear Isabelle's laughter, from where she was standing by the canal, but all she could see of the child were two small arms clutching round her father's neck, hanging on for dear life.

The human horse with its young jockey reached the spot where Becky was waiting smiling curiously at them both. Mr Hardy swung Isabelle around his back and swiftly down to the ground and then tried to catch his breath.

"Oh dear! I'm not as young as I used to be," he said, sucking in deep breaths of air. "I'm glad I caught you young Becky. We've got a very large delivery coming in today and we could really do with having someone to watch Isabelle. I can see that you're off into town but I wonder if you don't mind taking her with you. I know she'll be safe with you."

"Of course Mr Hardy, that's fine. I'm just going to the market and then I might watch the London train come in. Isabelle will probably enjoy watching the engine. I always do."

"Thank you, Becky. That sounds wonderful."

Ron Hardy bent down to give his daughter a kiss goodbye and then Becky took the little girl's hand and led her off towards the market. When they reached the marketplace Becky made her way over to where the Hayneses had their vegetable stand. As she approached she could see David was standing behind the stall, waiting to serve customers.

Becky's pace slowed down a little. She hadn't seen David since the accident as he had spent some time at home resting. Amy had told her that his face looked *'absolutely revolting'* and Becky was now nervous of what she was about to see. Taking a deep breath, she walked over to the stand.

"Hi David."

"Nurse Becky!" he said, looking up from the potatoes he was sorting.

Becky didn't reply. Her gaze was fixed on his right cheekbone. Although most of the swelling had gone and it was almost back to the normal size, nearly half of David's face was still a purplish, blue colour from the bruising. There was also a large black scab covering where the cut had been. His appearance startled Becky and she didn't know what to say.

Becky's eyes darted away from the wound.

"I'm sorry. I just didn't expect you to look so, so...."

"Ugly!" shouted Amy.

"Thank you little sister," retorted David, trying painfully to smile at her but then frowning because it hurt so much.

"It's okay Becky. I know I look quite awful but don't worry, Doctor Woodhouse says I'll be back to normal in a few weeks. But hey, never mind me. Has Amy told you her exciting news?"

Becky spun around to look at her friend with an eager expression of anticipation on her face.

"Oh don't look so intense Becky," she said, looking down at her feet. "It's actually not exciting at all. In fact I think it's absolutely boring!"

"Well?" asked Becky.

"Father is sending me to school."

The statement was made without feeling and Amy let out a quiet but defiant sigh to show her disapproval of the decision.

David explained, "It's all because of this business with Officer Webb. I finish school in a few weeks so Father said that we may as well continue paying the fees and send Amy. She can learn to read and write and what not and there'll be no more threats from George Webb."

"Oh yes!" squealed Becky. "And then you can teach me to read and write. Yes Amy, this really is exciting news."

Becky had always wanted to go to school, it was something she often dreamed about but never dare mention to her father.

"Well that's the only good thing about it," Amy replied, still sounding grumpy. "Personally, I don't want to learn to read. I just want to help on the farm."

Sensing that her friend was getting upset, Becky hastened to change the subject.

"Well, I promised Isabelle that we could go and look at the train. Are you coming with us?"

"I suppose so. I'm not allowed to sell vegetables, so I'm no use staying here."

"Yes please, take her away. She's far too miserable," called out David as the three of them set off in the direction of the station.

By the time they had reached the station in Merton Street Amy had cheered up. She and Becky had swung Isabelle high up into the air between them while they had been walking and the little girl's laughter was infectious. Amy soon forgot about feeling grumpy.

The train from London had not yet arrived but there were plenty of people stood around the platform waiting. Some were there to collect or see off passengers while others, like the three girls, were there simply to watch. The railway had been running through the town for a few years but the notion of travelling on the trains as passengers was a privilege that was only available to those with money. To Becky and Amy train travel was an experience which they could only dream about. They enjoyed watching the passengers getting on and off when the trains stopped on the platform. They especially enjoyed creating stories about who each person was and what business they were attending to.

"Let's go and stand over there." Becky pointed to a spot further down the platform. "There are less people so we will have a better view of everything."

They made their way down the long platform, away from the top end where the engine would stop and all the people who were standing there waiting. Passing the area where the horses and carriages stood parked, Becky noticed that her Uncle Tom was waiting to collect Mr Hamilton from the train. She waved at him but he didn't see her. He was busy talking rather animatedly to another driver. Standing closer than was usually polite to the man and with his arms gesturing all over the place, it appeared to any onlookers to be a lively conversation. Aware of her uncle's temperament Becky shook her head and continued walking.

As they stood waiting for the train to arrive Isabelle practised making noises like an engine and Becky and Amy joined in with the little girl's game.

Just a few minutes later and a loud blast from a train's whistle was heard in the distance and everyone on the platform stopped what they were doing and looked expectantly down the tracks.

Becky lifted Isabelle up into her arms and pointed at the sky. Giant puffs of white smoke were rising up from behind the factories to the south of the platform.

"Look Isabelle, the train is coming. Can you see the white clouds? That's steam from the engine."

"Yes," replied the little girl. "Choo, choo."

Isabelle was heavy so Becky let her back down to the ground and made sure to hold her hand.

Just a few moments later, another deafening blast on the whistle and the great engine appeared chugging along the tracks, pulling its beautifully painted carriages behind it. Isabelle started to jump up and down with excitement so Becky tightened her grip on the child's hand.

As the train came closer, the noise from the steaming engine got louder and louder until it passed by where Becky, Amy and Isabelle were standing and came to a halt at the north end of the platform. There it let out a long, loud hiss of steam. The platform was covered in white smoke and, finding it amusing, the three girls laughed loudly whilst fanning the air in front of them.

As the white fog started to clear and the doors on the carriages began to open, Becky and Amy's imaginations leapt into life.

Not far from where they were standing a middle-aged man painfully made his way out of the train leaning heavily upon two sticks. A young boy and girl ran to meet him while their mother stood watching with tears in her eyes.

"Look Becky. He has been away at sea for many

months. The ship was wrecked and he was presumed dead. However, he did not die. By some miracle he survived and now he is returning home to his family, never to sail again!"

Isabelle stared at Amy and then looked back at the family Amy had pointed to as she had been talking. They were all hugging each other. Isabelle started clapping her hands together happily, moved by Amy's dramatic story. Becky looked down at the little girl and smiled.

Further down the platform a young woman wearing a smart coat exited the train and was greeted by a young man in a tweed jacket. They stood embracing for a while on the platform's edge.

"Okay Becky. It's your turn," said Amy.

"She is from a rich family and he is a farmer's son," she started. "They were childhood sweethearts. Sadly her family did not approve and sent her away to live with her grumpy, old grandmother. For years she was trapped in the house. Now, at long last, she has escaped and returned here to marry him."

Isabelle again began clapping and the two older girls stood giggling.

"Oh look over there Becky. It's Mr Hamilton," pointed Amy. "But I can't see your uncle anywhere."

"No, nor I," wondered Becky and glanced over to where the horses and carriages stood waiting. In amongst the carts and carriages she could see that many of the drivers were standing in a circle. They were cheering and clapping loudly and the commotion was beginning to draw the attention of others who were making their way over to see what was happening. Becky's eyes searched through the heads, trying to spot her uncle but she couldn't see his thick red hair anywhere. She quickly looked back down the platform at Mr Hamilton who had picked up his bags and was now starting to walk towards the carriages. If Uncle Tom was getting into a pickle the last thing he needed was Mr Hamilton knowing about it.

Becky took Isabelle's hand and placed it quickly into Amy's.

"Please take her back to Mr Hardy for me. I have to stop Mr Hamilton from going over there."

Amy didn't have a chance to reply. Becky was already making her way hurriedly along the platform to get ahead of Mr Hamilton. The train had been busy and there were a large number of people leaving the station. Becky however, being lithe and petite, wriggled easily between everyone. Once ahead of Mr Hamilton she stopped and waited for him to approach. When he got near she boldly stood out in front of the short, balding man and held out her right hand.

"Good morning Sir. How do you do?"

Although an important businessman, Mr Hamilton had a friendly character and he didn't allow wealth and class to affect his good-natured personality. Amused by Becky's formal greeting he shook her hand by way of reply.

"Well, good day young lady. And to whom do I owe

this acquaintance?"

Her cheeks flushed red as she felt slightly embarrassed at being addressed as a *lady*. She was a mere twelve years old, just a child by all opinions. However, her thoughts were too preoccupied with the unfolding actions of her uncle to allow this unusual compliment to distract her. "My name is Rebecca Bailey Sir. I don't know if you remember me but I am Rose Watkins' niece."

"Of course I do. Your mother used to work for us when she was not much older than you are now. Well your uncle should be here somewhere to collect me. Are you here with him?"

"No Sir. Umm, yes. Well, I mean..."

As Becky desperately fumbled for words Mr Hamilton heard the cheering and clapping from over by the carriages and took a step forwards, towards the growing crowd of people.

"Wait," said Becky feebly. She had come over to try and deter Mr Hamilton from noticing the commotion, to stop her Uncle Tom from getting into trouble and to prevent her Aunt Rosa from all that would result, but she had no plan and now Mr Hamilton was heading towards the crowd.

"Please Sir, wait," she feebly called after him.

But it was no use. He wasn't listening to her. He continued heading in the direction he was walking. Becky stood there sadly, her hands hanging down by her sides, wondering what to do. Then there was a shout.

"Someone go for a Doctor."

"Oh no!" Becky ran over to the crowd and pushed her way through. As she reached the centre she gave a gasp but didn't know if it was of shock or relief.

In front of her was a man lying motionless on the ground with blood flowing from his nose, but this man wasn't her uncle. Tom Watkins was standing by the side wiping his own bloody face with his shirt sleeve.

As people moved in to attend to the injured man, police officers arrived and forced their way through the crowd then dragged Tom Watkins away.

Looking around hopelessly Becky caught Mr Hamilton's eye. He was frowning deeply at Tom Watkins as he was pulled from the area. However as Mr Hamilton's eyes met with Becky's and he read the fear and distress on her face his frown softened and a feeling of sympathy came over him. Still frightened and now confused by the look on the influential man's face she immediately turned away from the crowd and ran out of the railway station towards the Whately Coaching Inn and Aunt Rosa. She was anxious to arrive there before Mr Hamilton did.

5

It was early evening by the time Becky arrived back at the lockhouse. The sun, although sitting lower in the sky, was still shining and the air was beginning to cool a little. A few carefree birds were singing happily in the trees and Fidget was contentedly chasing his tail around in circles down on the tow path. A heavily loaded barge was just leaving the lock, heading north towards Warwick while Jim Bailey waited patiently to close the gate after it. Mr Dickenson was handing over several shovels of coal to the driver of the barge in exchange for a new cap that the driver's wife had picked up in London. Becky though, was too tired to take notice of any of this.

....

After leaving the station she had run as fast as she could all the way to the Coaching Inn and had passed on to Aunt Rosa the little information that she knew about what had happened. Usually Aunt Rosa was annoyed with Uncle Tom and seemed indifferent to his troubles. Moreover, usually Uncle Tom ended up injured to the same extent if not more so than the foolish person that he had been fighting with. But today was far from usual. Today it had all ended differently. Today, Tom Watkins had beaten a man unconscious and he was now sitting in a police cell. Today Aunt Rosa didn't get annoyed, she didn't even continue kneading dough, or slicing carrots impassively. Instead, she put down her knife, took off her apron and, as Becky finished talking, Aunt Rosa sat down. Her eyes welled up with tears and she started to cry.

Becky didn't know how to react. She had never seen her fearless Aunt Rosa look sad before. The kitchen girls carried on working, looking over their shoulders discreetly to try and see what was going on. As Becky stood uncomfortably by the table, desperately trying to think of something appropriate to say the door connecting the main house to the kitchens opened and Mr Hamilton walked in. One by one the half a dozen girls who were working in the room moved quickly and quietly away from the kitchen out to the parlour, taking their knives and ingredients with them. Becky's heart instantly sank further. Aunt Rosa was upset as it was and now here was Mr Hamilton, come to complain at her. This was the last thing poor, sweet Aunt Rosa needed. And yet, as Becky watched him close the door, she felt that maybe her expectations of him had been false. She noticed that he moved softly and calmly. When he turned to address them both, Becky could see that he was wearing the same expression on his face as he had when he last looked at her back at the station. His eyes were regarding Aunt Rosa, full of sympathy and compassion. As Mr Hamilton gently began speaking, Becky felt a wave of relief come over her.

"Alright there Rose, I can see the young girl has told you what has happened," he said, walking over and placing his hand comfortingly on Aunt Rosa's shoulder. "I spoke to one of the officers and Tom may be held for a while. Depending on how the other fellow recovers, or doesn't, there may be a trial. Now, now Rose," he continued as Aunt Rosa buried her face into her hands. "I don't want you to worry. Young Joshua is old enough and capable enough to drive the carriages and I don't expect it will make all that much difference to you whether Tom is around the house or not over the next few days."

Aunt Rosa looked up at Mr Hamilton and forced a half smile. The Hamiltons were under no false illusions about Tom Watkins. They knew he was a lazy man who did nothing to help his hard-working wife but they tolerated him working for them because they were fond of her. They were prepared to do anything that was needed to look after Rose Watkins, one of their most valued employees.

"Thank you Sir," replied Aunt Rosa. "My wayward husband would be the ruin of Joshua and me if it wasn't for your generosity."

"Well, you're a good woman Rose." he said opening the door that led out to the yard. "I'll go and see young Joshua. You have a cup of tea and settle your nerves again."

With that he left the kitchen. Becky stood staring after him with a look of amazement on her face. Aunt Rosa dabbed her nose and looked up at the girl.

"The Hamiltons are good people," commented Aunt Rosa.

"I couldn't believe it! He was so kind," replied Becky. "He's not at all what I would have expected of someone so important. But Aunt Rosa, are you going to be okay?"

"Me? Yes, of course," she answered, getting up from her chair putting her apron back on. "Well, let's have a cup of tea like Mr Hamilton said."

Becky spent a few hours with Aunt Rosa, helping her and the other staff to prepare the evening meal for Mr and Mrs Hamilton. When it came time for her to leave, Aunt Rosa gave her some odds and ends of food to take home for dinner and thanked her niece for keeping her company.

"I enjoyed having you here this afternoon dear," she said as they hugged goodbye. "Would you mind just not mentioning any of this to your father? I know he'll find out before too long, but I'd rather it wasn't today."

"Of course," said Becky, understanding the bad feelings that there sometimes were between Uncle Tom and her father.

....

Becky waited until the barge had left the lock and her father had closed the gate before crossing the canal and walking towards the lockhouse. Her father was also walking over towards the house. She approached quietly.

"Evening Father," she said.

"Huh."

He barely looked up at her. Becky sighed to herself. Well at least he wasn't going to ask her about her day. Becky's eyes glanced up and down the canal. Apart from the one barge that had just left the lock, there was no other movement on the water.

"It seems quiet."

"Silent you mean Rebecca. Silent!" He sounded vexed and Becky immediately wished she hadn't tried to start the conversation.

He continued, "There's a fault at Napton. I've barely seen a thing all day."

Napton was a set of nine locks further up the canal. Anyone coming down the canal with goods from Birmingham had to go through them. There were often hold ups there if the canal was busy and even if it wasn't it would take boats quite a few hours to go through them all. Today one of the locks had broken and needed repairing. Not a single barge or boat had been able to pass through the locks.

"Well surely they'll have it fixed by the morning," Becky stated brightly, hoping to lighten her father's mood a little. She was well aware that his way of coping with his misery in life was to keep busy and he hated to be idle, left to his own thoughts. As the wistful words left her mouth his jaw clenched tightly and she knew she had said the wrong thing.

"No Rebecca. It won't be fixed by the morning. Ron Hardy got word that the job's too much for the man at Napton. They'll have to wait until someone with more experience arrives from Birmingham." He was red in the face and Becky couldn't face an evening of bitterness.

"Well Father," she suggested hesitantly. "If you've got a quiet day tomorrow, I could stay at home and help you with the chicken shed."

She hoped he would approve of her idea and that it would take his mind away from the empty lock behind her. The chicken shed was in desperate need of repair and he had been complaining about it for weeks. If she was lucky he may even regard her idea as wise and sensible.

Jim Bailey looked back at his daughter with a blank expression. As she let out another little sigh and turned to go into the house when he answered her. "Good idea Rebecca."

Stepping forwards with her back already turned and away from his eyesight she smiled a little.

"But you can forget about helping me. You'll only get in my way."

Becky didn't allow her smile to drop. His praise of her suggestion was worth the happy feeling regardless of whether he wanted her there or not.

....

The information that Ron Hardy had been given proved to be accurate and not a single boat or barge came down the canal the following day. Word of the broken lock must have made it down past Oxford as no one bothered to come up the canal either.

Normally on a day like this Jim Bailey would be storming around with a big, black cloud on his shoulder. But today, thanks to Becky's suggestion he was almost agreeable. Busy repairing the dilapidated chicken shed Jim Bailey was content to still be doing a sort of work and achieving something.

Becky did her best to keep her father stocked up on tasty sandwiches and glasses of cool lemon cordial as well as keeping Fidget well out of the garden and away from where he was working.

At around four in the afternoon Ron Hardy strolled down to the house to let Jim Bailey know that the first boat had left Napton and would probably be coming through Banbury sometime the next day. To Becky's dismay Mr Hardy mentioned the fight that had occurred at the train station and commented on how lucky Tom Watkins was that the man's injuries were not as bad as they had first appeared to be.

When Mr Hardy returned home Becky waited for her father to start grumbling to her about her uncle's appalling behaviour but his day out in the garden had softened his temper a little and he said nothing to her about the whole matter.

That night Becky went off to sleep contented with Fidget curled up by her feet. She had enjoyed a peaceful day at home with her father and she felt reassured to know that Aunt Rosa didn't have the stress and fear of a trial hanging over her family.

6

By the beginning of July, summer had well and truly arrived and the inhabitants of Banbury enjoyed a pleasant air temperature as they went about their day to day business.

Becky loved this time of year and spent most of the days out on the tow path chatting to passers-by. She also made frequent outings to the Haynes' farm in order to spend time with Amy. As Amy was still not helping out a great deal on the farm the two young girls were able to please themselves.

One bright Wednesday morning it was particularly warm and Becky set off from home in the direction of the farm. Approaching the arch bridge she heard a whistle from up the hill. Looking up Becky could see that David and Amy were making their way down the field towards the canal. Waving frantically Amy started to skip buoyantly down to the bridge leaving David behind dragging some large brown object alongside him. Standing on the bridge, waving back at her friend, Becky could hear Amy shouting out to her but she couldn't quite make out what she was saying. Out of breath, the excitable farm girl reached the bridge and stood panting beside her friend and wiped the glistening beads of sweat from her tanned forehead.

"Oh Becky," she started, between gasps of breath. "I'm

so glad you chose to come here today! I was praying you would. We're going to have so much fun."

Amy was by now shaking her bewildered friend's arm while skipping around her in circles.

Becky started to giggle, bemused as ever by Amy's exuberant behaviour.

"What are you talking about?" she questioned.

"Father has just given us an old wheel from the cart. It's cracked in half but it will make a perfect seat for a swing. We're going to tie it up in a tree over the river. Isn't it great?!" she said, turning to look back up the hill where David was still laboriously making his way down to them. "Oh come on David. Hurry up!" she shouted. Then turning back to Becky she asked, "Well, what do you think?"

"It sounds wonderful," replied Becky. "But what if I fall in?" she added, looking down at her dress.

"Well, that's the whole point on a hot day like today. We can cool off and have fun. I'm going to play in my petticoat, it will soon dry off in the warm sunshine."

Becky glanced up the hill at David who was nearing the bridge now.

"Oh silly, don't worry about him," teased Amy. "He might as well be your brother too."

"And what a good sister she would make. I don't expect that our Becky here would leave her poor brother to carry this great heavy cart wheel all by himself."

As David joined the two girls on the bridge he let the big semi-circular piece of wood slip down from his shoulder to the ground and stood red-faced grinning at them both. Over five weeks had now gone by since David's accident and the bruising had disappeared. All that remained to remind him of the great power that is exerted by a horse's hoof complete with an iron horseshoe flying through the air were a couple of conspicuous, yet not too terrifying scars.

"So are you going to help us to build a rope swing Miss Becky?"

"I guess I am," she replied. "Although I don't know how to go about it."

"No, neither do I. That's why David is here," chirped Amy. "Well come on then. Let's go and pick our spot."

Becky and Amy together took hold of the thick heavy rope that David had been carrying on his back and the three of them continued over the bridge and through the field on the other side. When they reached the other end of the field and the grassy bank of the River Cherwell, David turned left and led the girls to a large tree that he had already decided on for their little project.

"Now what do we do?" asked Becky as they all stood staring up at the thick foliage.

"Well one of us has to climb up and wrap the middle part of the rope tightly around one of those branches."

"I'll do it!" exclaimed Amy, eagerly stepping forwards

towards the tree.

"No you won't," David reached out and gently pulled her back. "You'll only fall and hurt yourself and then Mother will blame me. No, I'll do it."

Amy tried to protest but it was to no avail. David was not going to risk an accident. He threw the rope across his shoulder and began to climb up into the tree. When he was up a little way he called down to the girls.

"Which of the bigger branches stretches out best over the water?"

Becky and Amy stepped back from under the tree to get a better view. After they had agreed on an appropriate branch they shouted directions up to David while he shuffled along to the right point. He quickly tightened the rope around the branch and secured it firmly. Then, after instructing the girls not to let the rope drop into the water, he threw the two ends down for them to hold on to while he carefully made his way back along the branch and down the trunk to the ground.

It was a fairly awkward task tying the two ends of the rope onto the half cartwheel. Thankfully David had thought ahead and had bored out two holes at each end to tie the rope through, but the whole thing still took a lot of effort. The base of the cut off wheel had to hang above the bank or it would just catch and get stuck on the ground when they sat on it. Even though there was only half of the wheel's original weight to hold, Becky and Amy still struggled to lift the wheel up and keep it steady while David tied the ends of rope through. Eventually, after a few puffs and pants and a good bit of teamwork, the rope swing was ready for testing.

David had removed the spokes from the wheel so that they had a nice smooth, curved piece of wood to sit on.

"Well, who wants to go first?" he asked, holding the swing up high above the river bank.

"Oh me. Yes! I will." Amy was already throwing her dress to one side and reaching out to take hold of the seat of the swing.

"Okay. On you get."

David held the two ropes on each side of the seat steady while his sister jumped on and held tight.

"Ready?"

"Ready!"

She let out a little squeal of delight as the swing swiftly carried her out across the water.

"It's wonderful. It really is!" she cried out as the swing swung back and forth over the river. When the motion of the swing slowed up she took a breath and let herself drop into the water below. The River Cherwell was just a small river at the point where it flows past Banbury. In most parts the water was barely knee depth. The spot that David had specially chosen was a bit deeper though. When Amy stood up she was waist deep in the water.

"Ohh, it's cold Becky, but so refreshing! Come on, what are you waiting for?"

Becky nervously took off her dress and walked over to the swing in her petticoat. Even though it was true that David was like an older brother she still found it embarrassing for him to see her in her underclothes.

David reached out and took hold of the swing again and held it steady while Becky got on. Then, after pulling it back a little higher he gave it a gentle push and Becky glided out above the water.

"It's like I'm flying!" she exclaimed, thrilled with the experience.

Although the river's width was quite narrow, the distance between the two banks was enough to provide an exciting ride for the young girl of twelve years. With the breeze rushing through her hair, Becky closed her eyes and relished the feeling.

"Come on. Jump!" Amy impatiently watched Becky go to and fro over the water and wanted her to jump in.

Looking down and holding her breath Becky slid off the swing into the water. Seconds later she jumped up to the surface gasping.

"Oh. It really is cold!" she shivered, jumping up and down.

Like Amy and David, Becky was able to swim and she swam around a bit quickly trying to warm up. Betty had insisted that Becky learn to swim a few years earlier. Betty's nephew had died drowning in the canal as had many poor men, women and children who had never learned even a few basic strokes. So Betty, full of fear for the young child with no mother and an ignorant father, had patiently taught Becky to swim well enough to get to safety if she were to ever fall into the canal or any other body of water. It was Betty's firm opinion that everyone working on and living by the canal should learn this lifesaving skill yet sadly it was an opinion that others were not so passionate about. As a result there was a large amount of people on the canal that would simply sink beneath the surface if they were to ever fall in.

Next it was David's turn to have a go on the wonderful new swing. He took his shirt off and laid it on the ground. Holding the ropes firmly with each hand he pulled the swing back towards himself. Then, after jumping high into the air he aimed and successfully landed his feet onto the seat as the swing flew out away from the bank. The girls clapped in applause and then screamed as he sat down on the seat and suddenly pushed himself off and into the river, splashing them both with cold water.

The three of them continued playing in the river for quite some time, chasing and splashing each other as well as jumping in and out for rides on the swing. After an hour or so they all climbed out of the water and lay in the grass, allowing the warm midday sunshine to dry the glistening drops of water from their skin, hair and clothes. In the pockets of Amy's dress were two cheese and ginger chutney sandwiches made that morning by Mrs Haynes and they shared them out between themselves. Once they had eaten they laid back down to soak in the beautiful, warm rays of sunlight.

"Would anyone like to try a bit of fishing?" asked David, sitting up and looking along the river.

"Oh no, I couldn't. I'm so tired now," replied Amy. "I'm going to lay here and sleep a little."

"Fishing? But how?" inquired Becky. Looking around she couldn't see that they had any tools for catching fish with them.

David grinned back at her. "I'll let you in on a secret."

He made his way over to a tree next to the one that they had tied the swing to and climbed up to the first branch. Then putting his hand into a small hollow within the trunk of the tree he pulled out a rectangular chunk of wood which had fishing line wrapped around it.

"I always keep this here so I don't have to carry it around with me."

Unravelling the line, Becky could see that there was a hook on the end with a small bit of metal attached to it.

"The metal flashes in the water," explained David. "And the fish like it."

"Oh," Becky stared up and down, examining the narrow river. "Are there any fish in there?" she asked disbelievingly.

David laughed. "Of course there are. It may be a small river but there are lots of fish swimming around."

"Really? Can you show me?" she asked.

Amy heaved a loud sigh to express her boredom at their conversation and rolled over on the grass.

"Of course. Follow me."

David led Becky downstream a little to an area where the rushing water flowed into a calm pool.

"The fish will be over there, sitting in the quiet part," he said, pointing to a slow moving spot in the water that he was describing. "You need to throw the hook in gently and then pull it fairly quickly through the water towards you."

After demonstrating a few times he passed the wood and line to Becky. "There you are. You have a go."

"Okay. I'll try," she said hesitantly, taking hold of the wood.

A couple of times she threw the line too far and the hook hit the bank beyond the water however, after a while she started to get more used to it.

"Come on, let's try another spot," David led Becky a bit further along the riverbank and she aimed the hook for another, similar calm area of water. As she pulled the line back through the water a third time she felt a little tug on the end of it.

"Oh, that feels strange," she commented.

Spying the flash in the water on the end of the hook, David leaped into action.

"Keep pulling. Don't drop the line. You've got one Becky.... that's it.... well done... excellent... Now get it out the water onto the bank... Brilliant... Good job Becky!"

Becky stood with her mouth wide open staring from David to the fish, that was lying gasping in the grass, and back again.

"Well I never!" she said shaking her head in disbelief. "There actually was a fish in there."

"Of course there was," David replied. He was kneeling over the fish and taking the hook out of its mouth. "Becky, can you find me a short strong stick please?"

She hunted around and soon passed him a sturdy little stick. "What's it for?" she asked.

"Well I have to kill it."

"Oh," she sighed, a hint of sadness in her voice.

"It's kinder than just leaving it gasping," he added sensing her feelings.

"I see," Becky looked away as David held the wriggling fish firmly on the ground and lifted the stick up with his other hand. Then, with one sharp, forcible sweep of his arm, he knocked the fish solidly on the head and it was out of its misery.

David picked the fish up and holding it out with both hands he presented it to Becky. It was a beautiful little brown trout. The silvery colours in its skin were shining brightly in the sunlight. Becky looked at her catch, lying motionless in David's hands.

"What do I do now?" she asked.

"Well you take it home and eat it."

"Okay. But… umm…" she paused. "How?"

David laughed as he then explained, "For first thing, you need to cut his belly, right along the middle and scoop out all his insides. Next, after you've given him a wash, you'll need to cook him."

"I've never cooked a fish before but I'll do my best," she replied and took the fish from him. "Thank you," she added not wanting to sound ungrateful.

They wandered back to find Amy. She was jumping across the great big stepping stones that sat fixed into the riverbed so that people could cross to the other bank. She was singing happily to herself.

"So, did you catch any fish?" Amy asked them both as they approached.

"Yes," Becky replied, trying her hardest to sound excited about it.

"So why the sad face?"

"We killed it and now I've got to cut all its insides out and cook it."

"Oh Becky, you're such a town girl," teased Amy. "You'll be fine and it will taste lovely."

"I'm sure it will," she replied, holding the little fish clumsily in her hands. "I suppose I'd better get home and chop this poor thing up. Thank you for a wonderful day you two."

"You're welcome," said David, patting her gently on the shoulder. "We'll walk with you to the bridge."

7

It was late afternoon when Becky arrived back home. She quickly went through to the kitchen to cook her fish thinking to herself that it would be a good surprise for her father as Becky couldn't remember them ever eating fish before. It would be a real treat and a home caught one at that.

She spent a few moments getting the stove going and burning hotly, and then she turned her attention to the small creature that had only a few hours earlier been swimming around in the river. Becky took out a chopping board and long sharp knife from the dresser. After rinsing the fish in a little water she gingerly laid it on the board. Looking at its lifeless silvery eyes she shuddered.

"It's not really looking at you. It's dead," she told herself and picked up the knife.

She held the knife gently by the back of the fish's head just behind the gills, just as David had told her to and, after taking a deep breath, she sliced into the pink flesh.

"Oh dear... Oh no!" she gasped, rapidly turning the fish over and doing the same to the other side.

Well that's the worst bit done, she thought and put the head to one side for Fidget to eat later.

As Becky scooped out the red, bloody insides of the fish she had to keep holding her breath and looking away as the sight and smell made her stomach heave.

Eventually the fish was clean and ready for the pan. Becky took a knob of butter from the pantry and melted it in the hot pan and then gently fried the fish. Next, taking a little cream and some parsley from the garden, she made a tasty sauce to go with it.

Hearing her father close the front door and take off his boots, she quickly cut the fish and put it onto two plates along with some potatoes and the sauce. Placing the meal on the table Becky felt a sense of inner pride. She had caught, prepared and cooked a beautiful new meal for them both. She felt a sense of achievement and satisfaction. As she carefully placed a knife and fork beside each plate Jim Bailey entered the room. Becky turned to face him. She couldn't contain her joy and her bright smile beamed at him.

Jim Bailey though, wasn't looking at his daughter. He was cautiously sniffing the air and looking around the room. Then his eyes came to rest upon the two plates that were sitting on the table, waiting to be eaten.

"Fish?" he grunted, now turning his attention to his daughter.

Becky's smile dropped. "Yes Father," she replied.

"I don't like fish."

He didn't move. His eyes just stared unemotionally at Becky.

"Well this isn't *just fish*," she started to explain. "You see, this is trout. It's special. I caught it. I..."

"*I* don't want it," he interrupted her and took a plate from off the table.

"But we've never had fish before, we always eat chicken. Please try it Father. I cooked it all especially...."

Becky stopped talking. Her father was walking towards the sink with his plate in his hand. He picked the piece of fish off the plate and threw it hard, into the sink.

"I don't eat fish!"

Without another word he left the room carrying his plate of potatoes with him.

For a moment Becky didn't move. Then as a tear rolled gently down her warm, sunburnt face she lifted a hand up to wipe it. Slowly, Becky sat down at the table in front of the solitary plate of food, facing an empty chair. Her small hands shaking a little, she lifted up her knife and fork and began to eat her dinner.

The flavours started to swim around inside her mouth and although Becky was conscious that it tasted good she didn't enjoy eating her meal. Instead she ate sad and alone, wiping the continuous stream of tears from her cheeks.

Jim Bailey didn't enjoy his meal either. As he ate his way through the plate of potatoes he could hear the quiet sobs that were coming from the kitchen. Small stabs of guilt began to attack him and his mood turned deeper and blacker. He finished his potatoes and stormed his way outside hoping that the clear night air would calm his churning emotions.

Fidget jumped in through the window just as Becky was clearing away the dishes. She placed her father's piece of fish along with the head on a saucer and Fidget started eating.

Stacking the dishes away in the dresser Becky could hear the little cat purring loudly while his teeth crunched on the bones. At least someone enjoyed their meal that night.

8

The warm sun had a wonderful effect on the plants and trees over the summer months and by the end of August, Oxfordshire was overflowing with ripe fruit and vegetables.

Mr Bailey and his daughter had a good sized kitchen garden and they enjoyed a year round harvest of delicious, fresh food. However, nothing lasts forever and unless somehow preserved most goes to waste. Each year as the wild fruits around the country started to ripen, Becky would set out to collect as much as possible and then Aunt Rosa would help the girl to make jams, chutneys and all sorts of preserves.

It was the last market day of the month. The air was a little cooler than it had been in previous weeks and the ground was damp from a slight drizzle of rain that had fallen overnight. Becky pulled a cream knitted cardigan over her shoulders, picked up two large baskets from the pantry and set off to meet Amy.

Becky reached the bustling market and made her way towards the familiar spot where Mr Haynes had his stall. She easily slipped between the men and women who were milling around. Market day was the occasion when townsfolk and those from the surrounding villages met together and had the opportunity to share news and more often than not gossip. Wriggling her way through the crowds Becky was able to catch snippets of quite a few different conversations. Some were lamenting the late arrival of tools and equipment due to the problems there had been at Napton. Others discussed the advantages and disadvantages of the line of work that they were in. One group of women were even gossiping about a new pregnancy, and how 'the poor woman had enough young'uns as it was.' Becky moved quietly and unnoticed amidst the conversations, focused on meeting with Amy, until she heard something that made her stop in her tracks.

She was passing a group of men whom she recognised from the town. One of them mentioned the name Tom Watkins just as Becky went by within earshot. Hearing her uncle's name she paused, standing out of sight, curious to hear what the men were saying.

"Well it's about time he got some penalty for his actions," she heard a bearded man say.

"If you ask me, a fine isn't anywhere near enough," a second man continued. "He should serve a stint in the gaol."

"At least he won't be able to afford to come out drinking for a while. We should get some peace for a few weeks. We should better..."

As the bearded man was talking two small boys ran through the crowd and knocked against his legs. He turned to look around and caught Becky's eye. He frowned, thinking it was Becky who had bumped past him.

"Get on with you. You pesky little thing!" he shouted,

waving his fist and Becky quickly moved on concerned by what she had heard.

Once Becky had found Amy the two girls made their way through the market and headed west, out of town. It was still fairly early and the road was busy with people heading towards the market. As they walked, the two friends talked together companionably. Their discussion turned towards the Parish school classes that Amy would soon be starting.

"It's just not fair. I'd much rather be at home helping Mother and Father," she complained.

"Amy please don't moan so much about it. I'd love for Father to send me to school. I can't read or write. I know nothing about geography or history. *You'll* learn so much."

Amy felt bad. She had been selfishly lamenting her own feelings and hadn't taken into consideration how Becky felt about this. Linking arms with her friend she apologised, "I'm sorry. I get too wrapped up in myself. You're right. It will be great. And what's more I will be able to teach you all the things I am learning."

"I'd like that," smiled Becky. "Okay, now what are we walking all this way for again?! Oh yes, I remember... blackberries! Maybe we should stop talking and start picking."

It was early in the season but the heavy spring rains and warm summer sun had ripened the blackberries a little earlier than usual this year. The hedgerows were full of big purple juicy berries just waiting to be picked. The girls hunted through the brambles, carefully choosing the best looking blackberries for themselves. Their baskets started to fill as they moved from one hedgerow to another in search of more fruity treasure. They weren't alone in their quest however. Many various insects had also been enticed out to gorge themselves on the sweet fruit. As they were picking the girls battled with flies, bees, and spiders to claim their prize. They stretched out to reach farther and higher in an attempt to get the best looking, unspoiled berries, whilst all the time avoiding the thorny spikes that the brambles used in a vain attempt to deter predators. Nevertheless, from time to time the girls heard each other yell out, 'Ouch!' and 'Ahh!' as the prickles attacked at them. Then a groan was heard from Becky.

"Oh why did I foolishly choose to wear cream?"

Amy turned to see that Becky's purple stained fingers had wiped against the side of her cardigan leaving an unsightly mark on the pearly coloured wool.

"Makes a change *your Ladyship.* It's normally clumsy old me that does things like that."

They both chuckled at the truth in Amy's statement then Amy put her basket down on the ground and let out a sigh.

"Do you think we have enough? I'm getting bored."

Becky tilted her head to one side with a mocking look of disapproval. "I've never known anyone as impatient as you."

"But Becky, we've been picking for ages and we've

walked miles. I see we're at Broughton already."

They both stood and looked down the hill at the hamlet of Broughton. In the foreground they could see the tiny village. There was a stone wall behind the village and on the other side they could just see part of the castle in the distance.

"What a wonderful life; all that land and that great big house to live in," Becky said jealously.

Amy looked at her friend and shook her head. "All that stuffiness to go with it too; walk in a certain way, sit in a certain way, speak in a certain way. No playing on swings in the river or picking blackberries for them."

"No you're right," agreed Becky. "But it must be a calm peaceful life that the ladies and gentlemen of this world live."

"Father always says, 'gentleman or lady, man or woman, lord or farmer, rich or poor – everyone's got troubles and stress.'"

"I expect that's true. But I'd still like to be a rich young lady all the same."

"Oh but you are Becky. You're a young lady with a purse full of treasure," laughed Amy, walking in the finest manner she could and holding her basket out in front like a posy.

"No, I'm a child with a handful of berries and a ruined cream cardigan," Becky smiled back at her. "Come on then. Let's get this lot to Aunt Rosa, she's expecting us."

The girls arrived back at the Whately Coaching Inn tired, hungry and thirsty. Aunt Rosa had indeed been expecting them. Lunch upstairs was finished and most of the kitchen staff were in the wash-up room or the pantry tidying things away. Aunt Rosa had laid the large kitchen table out with fresh salad, warm bread and a glass of cool cordial each. Becky saw that the pots, pans and dozens of empty jars were set out and waiting to be used.

"It's a good thing we picked plenty of blackberries Aunt Rosa. I didn't realise you had so many jars to fill."

Aunt Rosa smiled at them but Becky noticed that the usual glint in her eyes was not there today. She recalled the conversation she had overheard earlier in the market and again felt concerned.

The girls finished their lunch and then set about gently washing all the berries. As they washed, to Amy's surprise, little ants and other small creatures fell out of the blackberries and floated off down the sink.

"Urgh. I ate quite a few while we were picking. Do you think I ate ants and things?"

"Most probably," Becky giggled.

One of the kitchen girls got the large stove going hot and stood the pans of water on top to bring to the boil. Once the girls had finished they added the washed berries to the boiling water while Aunt Rosa weighed out the sugar to add to it.   Then they stirred and stirred until the mixture went to the correct thickness and consistency.

"Perfect!" declared Aunt Rosa, testing it with the back of a spoon and began to bring the jars over. The three of them had a great system; Becky spooned the hot jam into the jars while Amy sealed each one with a cloth and tied it securely. Finally, Aunt Rosa attached a label to each jar; 'Blackberry Jam. August 28th 1860.' The kitchen girl who had earlier stoked the stove went between Amy and Becky making sure that they were okay with what they were doing. In total they made twenty eight jars of jam. Aunt Rosa put sixteen in the pantry for the Coaching Inn and left six for each of the girls.   Becky would keep one or two for herself and her father but the others she would try to sell on the canal over the next few weeks.

They had just sat back down, pleased with all that they had accomplished when they heard David calling for Amy from the yard.

"That's Mother and Father ready," Amy jumped up and gathered her jars of jam together. "I told them to call for me here on their way home.   Thank you Mrs Watkins. Bye Becky."

Aunt Rosa waved Amy off with a cheery smile. As she closed the door, Becky saw that for a moment her smile dropped and her Aunt Rosa looked weary and tired.   Then, as she turned back round to face the kitchen and Becky her smile reappeared. Becky was worried by this unnatural smile, it reminded her of the smile that she often forced onto her own face when things were not so peaceful at home. Becky didn't feel though that it was her place to pry into Aunt Rosa's feelings.

She sat quietly for a while, thinking over her concerns, as Aunt Rosa and the girl who had helped tidied away the pots and then she stood up.

"Well I'd better get back now. Thank you for letting us make the jam here."

"No dear, thank you for picking all the berries. It saved me the time and effort."

Becky nodded and turned to go.

Aunt Rosa caught her arm. "What are you worried about dear? You've looked fretful since Amy left."

Becky looked down at her feet. "Well actually, I'm a little worried about you," she whispered, so that the kitchen girl wouldn't overhear her.

Aunt Rosa held Becky's chin in her hands. "Well, you mustn't worry. I'm fine."

"But I heard some men saying things about Uncle Tom and you look so tired, I..."

"Really Becky, I'm fine. But thank you for worrying. Now off you go, your father will be getting hungry."

Becky headed back to the lockhouse, her brow furrowed into a deep, fretful frown and feeling dissatisfied with what Aunt Rosa had told her.

Aunt Rosa waved her goodbye, shut the door and

ONE FINE LADY

wiped a tear that had escaped from her watery eyes.

<u>Autumn</u>

1

The first day of September was fine and dry. After finishing her jobs at the lockhouse Becky made her way up to Robinsons' butchers to buy some fresh sausages for the meal that evening. As she approached the busy shop she saw that Mr Hamilton's personal carriage was just pulling up on the opposite side of the street. Her Uncle Tom was driving; however he did not notice her across the road as he was too busy admiring two attractive young women that were walking past where the carriage had come to a halt. When they had passed he then apparently remembered what he was in fact doing and quickly jumped down and ran around to open the door to the carriage. Tom Watkins was hidden from Becky's view behind the carriage as he opened the door nearest to the pavement. She was however, able to see under the carriage as the feet and legs of Mr Hamilton stepped down onto the ground. About to turn to go into the butcher's shop Becky noticed a pair of women's feet also stepping out of the carriage onto the pavement followed by a small pair of girl's feet and finally those of another gentleman.

Becky was interested now and watched as the four passengers came into view from behind the carriage and walked along the pavement towards Dobsons' tailor shop. Becky could now see that Mr Hamilton was accompanied by a tall thin man, a younger woman and a girl about the same age as herself. They were all dressed quite nicely and looked far too neat and tidy for the small country town. Becky had never seen them before and wondered who they were. Then Mr Hamilton opened the door to the tailor's and they all followed him inside.

Becky had to wait for a while in the butcher's before she was served as it was very busy inside. After quite some time patiently queuing she chose eight fat sausages to take home for tea. Stepping back outside she saw that the carriage was still parked across the street and that her Uncle Tom was now standing up the road having a smoke and a chat with a fellow driver.

Still curious about the identity of the three visitors, Becky made her way to Browns' bakery to get some bread. It was much quieter in the bakery than it had been at the butcher's and she was soon opening the door and stepping back out onto the pavement. Becky walked out of the door and straight into Aunt Rosa.

"Becky dear! Well fancy seeing you today," gasped Aunt Rosa.

"Oh, I'm so glad I've bumped into you..."

"You mean *collided!*" teased Aunt Rosa.

"Yes, sorry," she apologised. "It's just that there's something I have been wondering about."

"Yes dear?"

"Well I've just seen Mr Hamilton come into town with

some visitors that I've never seen before and they look quite 'well to do', not like they come from round here, and I was wondering who they are?"

"Oh, I thought Mr Hamilton was showing them the sights not shopping in town, how strange," she commented, her eyes looking around as if expecting to see them.

"Aunt Rosa, please tell me."

Aunt Rosa looked again at her niece and frowned. "You are such a nosey, impatient child...okay, I'll tell you who they are; they are Mr Hamilton's brother-in-law and niece. They arrived from London only two days ago."

"There was a woman with them too. Is that Mr Hamilton's sister?"

"A woman? Ah, no. That would be the child's governess. Although from what I've heard of her from the staff upstairs, she is of the opinion that she is of higher station than a governess. The mother is sick in London, I believe, and the father has to go north soon for business, so the girl and her governess have come to stay at the Coaching Inn for a few weeks. I haven't met them yet, and don't expect I will."

"Well, imagine having a governess. That would be wonderful. That beats even Amy going to school. I do wish..."

Aunt Rosa didn't get to hear what it was that Becky wished as at that moment the party of four came around the corner and Mr Hamilton spotted them both.

"Rose! I'd have thought you would have left town before now," he exclaimed. "However, I'm glad we have caught you. I meant to ask you to pick up some Banbury Cakes. We are just on our way to get them ourselves as I'd forgotten to request it. James here hasn't had one for years and is just dying to taste one again."

"Well I would have been halfway back to the inn by now Sir, except that I just ran into my niece here."

"Yes, of course. I've met you before, haven't I? It's Rachel isn't it?" he said, addressing Becky.

"Umm, actually it's Rebecca, Sir," she replied politely. It always surprised Becky that Mr Hamilton was so friendly to everyone considering he was quite a superior figure in the town.

"Almost! I knew it began with an 'R,'" he laughed. "James, Emma, this is Rose Watkins our head cook and her niece *Rebecca*," he said, introducing them to his visitors.

"Well then it's you we have to thank for last night's delicious meal," said the tall thin man. He stepped forward with a big smile and shook Aunt Rosa's hand. "I'm James Jenkins, Joseph's brother-in-law. This is my daughter Emma and also Miss Anne Cartwright."

Aunt Rosa could plainly see that despite Mr Jenkins' friendly greeting, Miss Cartwright clearly did not approve of introductions to kitchen staff in public, if at all.

"Quite," she nodded to Aunt Rosa, just about managing a half-smile before looking down to address an imaginary issue with her belt. A plain looking woman of about thirty years old, dressed in simple but well-tailored clothes she appeared unimpressed with everything and everyone around her.

Unaffected by her manner Mr Hamilton continued, "Well isn't it fortunate that we have run into Rose and Rebecca today?! Emma was only saying last night that she should love to see the town. Maybe young Rebecca could show her around."

It seemed to Becky that the girl standing opposite her wanted anything *but* to be shown around. Tall and gangly like her father she looked uncomfortable and self-conscious. She had been staring down at her feet during the whole conversation.

"Well Emma, what do you think?" pushed Mr Hamilton. Emma looked up. She was not a particularly pretty girl and had an unfortunate pointed nose. Her eyes met Becky's and she reluctantly smiled. Becky realized that she was painfully shy.

To help her feel at ease, Becky smiled back warmly. "I'd be very happy to show you around Emma."

"Well isn't that perfect," continued Mr Hamilton. "Now tell me, how old are you Rebecca?"

She beamed at him. Becky had turned thirteen a few weeks earlier but this was the first time anyone had enquired after her age since her birthday. She felt extremely grown up as she now replied, "I'm thirteen Sir."

"That is almost perfect. Emma will be thirteen in just a few months from now. I'll tell you what James, why doesn't young Emma go with Rebecca now, we can buy the cakes and then take the carriage back to the inn."

While Mr Hamilton was talking Becky noticed Miss Cartwright turn to Mr Jenkins with her nose held high and a look of contempt about her. Even though she was whispering to him, Becky could still hear her words.

"Mr Jenkins, Sir. I don't feel that it is wise to permit Emma to wander off with this... *servant girl*. Surely Mrs Jenkins would not approve."

Becky flushed pink and looked down at her appearance. Catching sight of herself she cursed inwardly. Becky had come into town, from the lockhouse that morning in order to run a few errands. She was wearing an old, tatty dress which she used to do her jobs as it was almost too small for her. She also had on her unpolished house shoes. Emma on the other hand was dressed very neatly in a navy frock with matching jacket, clean shoes and a stylish bonnet. Deeply embarrassed Becky realized that she must look a terrible sight.

Although talking, Mr Hamilton had also caught part of Miss Cartwright's words and he immediately corrected her.

"Indeed, I expect that my dear sister would not approve of Emma running off for the day with a servant girl but you see, Miss Cartwright, Rebecca is not a servant girl, nor is her father a servant. Mr Bailey is in fact the lock keeper. Come to think of it, I don't expect you have ever seen a lock or the canal have you Emma?"

"No, I haven't Uncle," replied Emma, still standing nervously by her father.

"Well there we go," announced Mr Jenkins, eager to support his brother-in-law. "Rebecca will make a very acceptable acquaintance and Emma will have a great time seeing new things. In fact, if it wasn't for all the paperwork I have to do before I leave tomorrow I'd have joined you both down to the lock to see it for myself."

Anne Cartwright had been standing with her mouth open about to add more arguments against this arrangement. However, as Mr Hamilton clapped his hands together and Aunt Rosa nodded happily she closed her mouth and an angry frown formed across her brow. Becky couldn't help but breathe a sigh of relief – as Mr Hamilton knew only too well, her own mother had indeed been a servant girl, and so would she be too if her parents had not married and her mother gone to live in the lockhouse.

"Right then, let's be getting on," continued Mr Hamilton. "Rose, you might as well ride home with us. It will save you carrying all that back. Why don't you show Miss Cartwright back to the carriage, it's by the tailor shop. James and I will pop in here for the cakes quickly." Winking at Becky as he turned to open the baker's door he added loudly, "It was delightful to see you again *Miss Rebecca*."

With a snort of disapproval, Anne Cartwright turned sharply to walk back to the carriage while Aunt Rosa followed at an awkward distance.

For the second time in only a few minutes, Becky flushed pink as she led Emma towards the canal.

2

Emma walked alongside Becky through the town to the canal. It was evident from Emma's stiff, uneasy movements and reluctance to make eye contact that she was feeling far from comfortable in the company of her new acquaintance. Becky tried to make up for the awkwardness by cheerfully pointing out places of interest along the way. By the time they reached the lock, Emma's shoulders had relaxed a little and she was beginning to acknowledge Becky's efforts to create ease.

Explaining the need to tread carefully, Becky helped Emma across the lock gate and over to the lockhouse. The lock was empty and as Becky looked around she saw that her father was a little way down the canal, clearing away a few overgrown reeds. He didn't notice as the two girls walked around to the back of the house and into the kitchen.

"Have a seat," offered Becky, motioning to the small table and two chairs. "I just need to put these things away in the parlour."

Emma nervously sat down and looked around at the small, simply furnished room with an old stove in the corner and a little sink by the window.

Becky looked back in from the parlour and asked, "Would you like a glass of water and maybe some bread and cheese? I'm feeling quite hungry myself."

"That would be nice, thank you," Emma quietly replied.

She watched as Becky brought out a knife and a large wooden board to cut some bread for the two of them. Becky took a couple of plates and some cutlery from the dresser and laid the food out for Emma and herself.

As they ate Becky broke the silence by explaining that she had helped to make this cheese at her friend Amy's farm. She went on to tell her in detail about the cheese-making process. Emma politely nodded but didn't press for more information.

Becky cleared the plates away and was beginning to wonder how this uncomfortable afternoon was going to continue when Fidget wandered into the kitchen and a little of Emma's nervousness subsided.

"Oh...you have a cat."

Becky was at the dresser and turned to reply. She could see that Emma's expression had changed. Her lips that had until now been tightly pursed together were relaxed and she was smiling freely.

"His name is Fidget. He loves having his belly tickled." Becky realized that she had to make the most of this opportunity. Something about Fidget's presence had relaxed Emma and Becky needed to prolong the moment.

Emma got up from the table and went to kneel next to

the cat. She stroked him gently and he started to purr. Then to Becky's amazement and relief, she started talking.

"I have a cat at home. Her name is Snowball. She's white. I miss her."

Feeling a little more confident now that she had spoken properly, Emma smiled up at Becky and again looked around the room.

"May I ask you a question?" she enquired.

"Of course," encouraged Becky.

"Do you not have a maid?"

Now it was Becky's turn to feel self-conscious. Her glance shifted down and she again caught sight of her clothes.

"Uhh...no..." she nervously replied. "It's just Father and I."

"So do you usually prepare the food and collect things from town?" Emma's tone contained no scorn or malice. She was simply curious.

"Yes," Becky answered, adding, "I also clean the house."

"You really do everything?! You mean that no one helps you?!"

Becky now started to look distressed.

"It's just that I wouldn't know where to start." Emma

could see she had been blunt. She quickly stumbled to explain, eager not to make Becky feel uncomfortable. "You see, I don't know a thing about cooking or lighting a stove."

"I've always done those things, as far back as I can remember," Becky replied. "Mother died when I was very young. Father is busy on the lock. So I do it all. Well not quite all. Betty comes to help with the washing."

"Is Betty a maid?"

"No, she lives up the canal. Father does pay her for her help though," Becky paused thoughtfully. "So...umm...do you have a maid?" she asked hesitantly.

"We have two."

Becky thought that she seemed a little embarrassed.

"Only one lives with us though," Emma added, "The other girl just comes in during the day.

"Oh, I see." Becky felt that Emma must be very rich.

"Of course that's nothing compared to Uncle Joseph and Aunt Caroline. They have dozens of maids and servants."

Emma smiled gently at Becky and Becky agreed with a small laugh. "Yes. Half the town works at the Coaching Inn."

Both the girls relaxed. It was clear to Becky that Emma hadn't meant anything by her comments. Like her uncle and her father, she wasn't snobbish. She just seemed interested in the differences that they both had in life as her next question showed.

"So if you don't mind me asking, how many rooms are in this house?"

There was a pause.

"Sorry, Father always tells me that I'm too nosey."

"No, it's fine," assured Becky. "There are only four, two downstairs and two upstairs."

"So your bedroom is upstairs is it?"

"Yes. Why don't you come up and see?"

"May I?!" Emma was eager to see more of the little lockhouse.

Becky led her up the narrow staircase and lifted the latch on her bedroom door. Emma walked in and looked around at the small room. Like the kitchen it was simply furnished. Becky had her bed, a wardrobe and a plain dresser.

"Did you draw those?"

Emma pointed to the wall above Becky's bed where some of her drawings were pinned up.

"Yes."

"I wish I could draw. I'm useless at anything like that."

Becky felt awkward, not used to hearing praise, and quickly changed the subject. "I have a lovely view of the canal from my window," she said, pointing to the window.

Emma stood by the window and looked out for a while.

"Is that your father?" she asked.

Becky looked down and could see her father outside by the lock. A boat was approaching from up the canal.

"Yes, that's him."

"So what does he do as a lock keeper?"

"Come outside and I'll show you. There's a boat nearly here. Just let me change out of my old clothes first."

The two girls arrived outside just as the boat came to rest in the lock. The owner of the boat travelled through regularly and he waved to Becky. Jim Bailey had closed the gate behind the boat and was walking down to the other gate with a long metal bar in his hand.

Emma stood back out of the way. She looked nervous again but was still interested in everything that was going on.

"What are they doing?" she whispered.

"Now that the boat is in the lock Father can let the water out the other end. That is the windlass he has in his hand. It's like a special key for the lock."

Jim Bailey was turning the windlass and Emma heard the water start to flow out of the lock.

"I don't understand. What does it do?"

"It's a bit like a step in a staircase," Becky explained. "Canals are flat but the land goes uphill and downhill so the lock takes the boat up and down. This boat wants to go downhill. Father is letting the water out down over there. If you step closer you can watch the water in the lock go down."

Emma stepped forwards and peered into the lock. As she watched the water level was indeed going down and the boat along with it. Two children inside the boat waved in the window as it disappeared from view. Emma shyly waved back.

"Who are they?"

"They are the children of the boatman. His wife is in there too."

"Do they all live on that tiny boat?"

"Yes," Becky realized that Emma was being introduced to a lot of new things today. "The whole family lives in there and the father transports goods up and down the canal."

"How interesting...I can't believe how deep the lock is!"

Emma was amazed. The boat was now well below them in the lock. She felt as if she could step off the side of the lock directly on to the roof of the boat.

"You see, it's like it's gone down a step. Now, when Father opens the other gate on the other side the boat will be level with the canal over there."

"I see. It's very wonderful. I've never seen anything like it before."

They waved goodbye to the children inside the boat as the hauler hitched the horse back up and it continued on down the canal. As Jim Bailey walked back towards them Becky thought she should introduce Emma.

"Father this is Emma Jenkins. She is Mr Hamilton's niece."

Whilst working the lock, Jim Bailey had noticed the girl's smart clothes and was a little surprised by her presence at the lockhouse. Emma was again struggling with her shyness and nervously held out her hand to Becky's father.

Unfamiliar with such formalities from children he disconcertingly shook her hand. Still puzzled as to why this well dressed girl was visiting his daughter he opened his mouth to question her. Before he was able to speak, a voice called to them from across the canal.

"Afternoon Uncle Jim."

All three looked over to see Joshua standing on the other side of the lock.

"I've come to collect Miss Jenkins, if she is ready," he explained. "I have Mr Hamilton's trap to take her in."

Emma looked horrified at the thought of being escorted by Joshua back to the Coaching Inn. Becky noticed the terrified look on Emma's face. She'd never known anyone so shy.

"I'll come too," she called out quickly. "I didn't finish

talking to Aunt Rosa earlier."

Becky heard Emma breathe a sigh of relief.

"I won't be long Father," she said crossing the lock.

"It was nice to meet you Sir," mumbled Emma, rushing after Becky.

Confused, Jim Bailey shrugged his shoulders and shook his head, mystified by this new acquaintance.

3

"So, for how long is she staying with the Hamiltons?" asked Amy.

"It could be until November," Becky replied.

They were cleaning out the two stables on the farm that housed Sparkle, the carthorse, and Star, the little pony. Their progress was slow as they had much to catch up on. Becky was explaining to Amy all about her meeting with Emma the day before.

"And exactly how much time is she going to spend with you?" Amy rested her pitchfork on the ground and lent on it. The tone in her voice was fiery.

Becky swept a stray strand of hair from her eyes as she stood upright to face Amy. "I really don't know. She may not even want to spend time with me."

"Of course she will!" Amy sounded indignant.

"Why are you giving me an inquisition?"

"I'm just showing interest. *Sorry* for being interested!" Amy turned back around and furiously poked at the soiled straw on the stable floor.

The truth was that she was feeling a little sensitive and slightly jealous.

After Becky had accompanied Emma back to the Coaching Inn and said goodbye, she had gone to the kitchen to see Aunt Rosa. While they were talking together Emma's father had come through to the kitchen escorted by Mr Hamilton. Becky still felt excited but a little apprehensive as she repeated the conversation they had together to Amy.

....

"Ah, good. We were hoping to catch your niece before she returned home Rose." Mr Hamilton had said.

"Indeed Sir? Is everything okay?"

"Yes, splendid." He turned and addressed Becky. "Rebecca, I wonder if Mr Jenkins and I could ask something of you?"

"Yes Sir?"

"You see, Emma's father is leaving in the morning for the North of England and will be away some weeks. My sister, Emma's mother, is at home in London recovering from a serious illness and so Emma has come to stay here to give her mother a rest. I was hoping that maybe you could spend some time with Emma, as a friend."

Mr Jenkins joined the conversation. "Emma has such a lonely life in London. I saw a glint in Emma's eyes that I've never seen before when she returned with you just now. I would be grateful if she could spend some time with you while she is here."

Becky was shocked. The day's events were becoming

more and more bewildering with every moment. To start with, this extremely shy and possibly quite rich girl had spent the afternoon with her in her small, extremely modest house and now she was being asked to spend time with her; to entertain her; to be her friend.

Mr Jenkins could sense Becky's surprise at this request. Emma had just told him about her simple house and of the work that Becky did to look after her father and herself. He hastened to assure her.

"I have it on good recommendation from my brother-in-law that you are a respectable and capable young lady and that I can fully trust my daughter in your company."

Becky's cheeks blushed pink while Aunt Rosa nodded proudly, beaming in approval.

"Besides, my daughter really likes you."

Becky smiled. back at him. "I would enjoy spending time with Emma."

It was true. Becky felt that if she could get past the shyness then Emma would be an easy-going person to have around.

"Excellent. She will be tutored by Miss Cartwright each morning from nine until noon. I cannot allow her to get behind with her lessons just because she is away from home. However, after lunch she may join you whenever it is convenient."

"Mr Jenkins Sir?" Aunt Rosa stepped in. "Becky lives a

very rural life. She often spends time at the market or on her friend's farm. I hope you won't object to Emma enjoying some of these activities."

Becky nodded. Aunt Rosa guessed correctly that she had been thinking of Amy's feelings about this new situation.

"Not at all," Mr Jenkins replied. "All she knows is her life in London. I want her horizons to be broadened and of course, the more children her own age she can interact with the better. She really does have a lonely life back home."

"Well that's settled then," declared Mr Hamilton, moving to leave the kitchen. "Just come to call for Emma whenever is best for you Rebecca. We all appreciate it."

After saying goodbye the two men left the kitchen.

......

Becky had carefully recounted all of this to Amy who was now reacting just as she had feared.

"Amy, please don't be like that. I asked specifically if she could spend time with you also."

"What if I don't want to spend time with '*Little Miss London,*'" Amy snorted.

Becky took a deep breath. "Well I sincerely hope that you do. She seems like a nice girl. I think we could have a lot of fun, the *three* of us."

She calmly looked Amy straight in the eyes hoping

that her friend would understand that she wasn't trying to hurt her.

Amy's defiant face broke into a reluctant smile. "Oh, okay. How bad can it be?!" She laughed and nudged Becky's shoulder reassuringly.

"Thank you," said Becky. "You know you'll always be my best friend."

4

The days swiftly flew by, September moved into October, and Emma became more at home in Banbury. She spent most of her afternoons in Becky's company, either at the lockhouse or somewhere else in the town. Emma spent as little time as possible at the Coaching Inn. Miss Cartwright would always try to find her something 'constructive' to do and it rarely involved Becky. Much to Becky's relief, Amy's jealousy was short-lived and within a few hours of meeting her, Emma relaxed and the three of them got on very well together. However, with Amy attending the school in Bodicote a few mornings each week and her living outside of the town she wasn't with the other two as much as she would have liked to have been.

As Becky had suspected, underneath Emma's nerves she was an extremely likeable companion. She was eager to see as much as possible of rural life and, in the company of her new friends, was keen to experience as many new things as she could.

"So what are Amy's family like?" Emma asked Becky as they hurried along the tow path towards the Hayneses' farm one bright Friday afternoon.

"Oh you'll definitely like them. They're very friendly."

"At least you and Amy will be there," Emma was still shy in unfamiliar situations. "Becky, just imagine if

Miss Cartwright were to see what I am wearing."

"Oh, if only she could!" agreed Becky.

Emma only had smart, neat clothes with her and her overbearing governess did not approve of 'play clothes.' Aunt Rosa had found some spare clothes in the servants store room at the inn and Emma was now wearing them so as not to ruin her good clothes on the farm. They were old, plain and a little too big but they would be perfect for the afternoon's activities.

"I hope we won't be late," Emma continued, "Miss Cartwright is such a bore."

They were making their way to the farm to help with the potato harvest. Emma had begged her governess to allow her one morning off her studies so that they could get to the farm earlier but she had flatly refused. Anne Cartwright was still extremely disapproving of Emma's association and her gallivanting about the town. However, Emma's father had made it very clear before he left that he wanted Emma to have this freedom and so, much to her annoyance, there was nothing she could do to prevent it. Nevertheless, her instructions were to give three hours of tuition each morning and this was something that she ensured was carried out precisely with no room for negotiations. Emma had considered asking her Uncle Joseph to intervene on this occasion but she knew only too well that if she went to him, Miss Cartwright would make her pay for it some other day.

"Well it will take days to harvest all the fields so don't worry, they won't finish without us," Becky assured her.

"Should we walk faster...just in case?" Emma asked skipping ahead.

"I don't feel as though my legs could go any faster," Becky despaired. It had been a long morning. Her father had been in a particularly bad mood and had complained about the state of the fireplace in the sitting room at the lockhouse. It hadn't been used during the warm summer months and he had gone to light it the previous evening and was frustrated to find it not raked out and unprepared for lighting. To keep him happy Becky had spent that morning clearing out and washing down the fireplace as well as bringing in kindling and logs, enough for a few days in advance. Now she was feeling quite weary.

They reached the arch bridge and made their way up the hill, through the field, to the farm. Emma had been excitedly walking ahead but as they approached and voices could be heard in the distance she dropped back, behind Becky and fell silent. Becky was used to this by now. Emma's timid ways returned every time she was introduced to someone new. Becky gave her an encouraging smile and they followed the sound of the voices into one of the large potato fields that were being harvested.

Walking through the open gateway, they came upon a flurry of activity. Emma had never seen the bustling sight of a field being harvested and she gazed open-mouthed at the unexpected scene in front of her.

"There are so many people!" she exclaimed.

There were about twenty people of various different ages all working tirelessly in the field. Becky thought about it and conceded that yes there was quite a number, especially considering that the Hayneses' farm was not particularly large.

"But why are there so many?" asked Emma. "Amy doesn't have a large family."

"Well the farmers and their families all help each other to get all the harvests in. Today a family or two may help Mr Haynes and then tomorrow or next week he will go over to help them in return." Becky looked around the field as she spoke. "And there may be one or two hired men here to help out as well," she added, not recognising a few of the faces.

"I didn't expect so many people to be here," Emma said anxiously. "Where is Amy? Can you see her anywhere?"

Becky's eyes searched across the field. "Yes. She's over there." She pointed to the far end of the field where a group of younger boys and girls were quickly collecting potatoes and placing them into large sacks, "I don't think she has noticed us yet."

Becky was correct. Amy had her back to them and was busy gathering up potatoes as fast as her arms would allow her. She hadn't noticed her two friends arrive. Someone else had though. David was working closer to the gateway. He was moving swiftly along one of the lazy beds using a special spade, with a longer than usual handle, to turn the soil over and dig the potatoes out from under the ground. He had caught sight of a

151

movement over by the gate from the corner of his eye and looked up to see the two girls stood side by side in the field.

To get Amy's attention, David placed his forefinger and thumb in behind his teeth and whistled loudly. Amy looked up immediately and also spotted Becky and Emma.

"Hey! Over here," she called, waving to them both.

Becky called out thank you to David as they headed across the field to join Amy. He had already resumed digging at the damp, clumps of soil and didn't respond.

"Who's that boy that whistled?" asked Emma.

"That's David, Amy's brother. You'll meet him later. It seems that everyone is too busy for introductions now."

"At last you're here!" exclaimed Amy. "I'm seriously outnumbered here by little'uns."

It was true. Working alongside Amy and at a visibly slower pace were three children all under the age of eight. They were all brothers and sisters and their father was one of the nearby farmers who were helping the Hayneses with their harvest. They were skinny little children with scraggly hair and their clothes, as well as any uncovered skin, were stained with brown mud and dirt. Emma couldn't help but notice the amount of soil that was also attached to Amy's clothes, hands and even her face.

"I hope you're not afraid of getting dirty Emma." Amy grinned, her teeth appearing unusually white next to her grubby face.

"No I'm not and it certainly looks as though that's what is going to happen to me," Emma replied, bracing herself for the work she was about to do.

"Will the *wonderful* Miss Cartwright object?" Amy teased.

"I expect so but thanks to Becky's remarkable Aunt Rosa, Miss Cartwright will never know."

"Brilliant!" laughed Amy. "Now let's get going or these babies I'm working with will show us up. Emma, do you know what to do?"

"I don't have the faintest idea."

"Well don't worry, it's not difficult. The boys are digging up the beds. This bed here has already been done as you can see. All we have to do is collect up all the potatoes. Mother has laid some sacks out up and down the beds. So what I do is make a cradle in my skirt here and carry a few potatoes at a time to the nearest sack."

"Now I understand why half the field is in your dress," said Emma, gathering up her skirt.

"Becky, why don't you work with the children and I'll help Emma?" suggested Amy.

Emma couldn't believe how hard they worked. It seemed to her that Amy was the strongest, fastest working girl she had ever met. Unused to lifting and carrying Emma felt quite weak and pathetic in comparison. Yet she struggled on, determined not to let everyone down. Before long her fingers and nails were clogged with dirt and her clothes were stained a muddy brown from the clammy soil that stuck to each potato. As strenuous as she found the harvest process to be, Emma was actually really enjoying herself. Turning to start collecting from a new bed of freshly dug potatoes she felt a satisfaction and esteem that she had never known before. It made her feel really good inside.

Although fatigued from her morning exertions, Becky was also getting on well. The young children she had with her were easily distracted but equally eager to please. Becky turned the task they were doing into a little game and happily, they piled the potatoes into the sacks. When their demeanour began to show boredom or fatigue Becky speedily changed to a new game and their enthusiasm began once again.

Emma didn't know how long they had been working but it felt as though an age had gone by before the girls heard a long, loud whistle. They looked up to see all the men resting around the large cart which was being used to collect the potatoes. Some of the stronger men had been going around emptying the heavy sacks into giant, big barrels which were sitting on the cart. Amy's mother was now handing out cups of cool water and beckoned all the young pickers over to join them.

They made their way over towards the other tired workers and as they approached this group of strangers, Becky guessed that Emma would be feeling nervous. Her assumption was correct. When Becky clambered up onto the cart to sit and rest her legs, Emma quietly climbed up and hid behind her. Amy brought over three cups of water and sat beside them.

The men were all talking about the harvest and how it was going. Mr Haynes was questioning another farmer about what he had heard of drill ridges, a new tool for digging out the potatoes, and whether he thought it would be worth investing in some in the future. The younger children were noisily playing a game of hide and seek around the cart. To Emma it was a happy scene.

Mrs Haynes finished handing out the water and came to sit beside the girls.

"So you must be Emma. I'm Mary Haynes, Amy's mother." She kept her voice soft and quiet so as not to draw attention from the others. Amy had warned her of Emma's shyness so Mrs Haynes was careful not to make the girl feel uncomfortable.

"Hello. It's nice to meet you." Although Emma struggled to make eye contact, her manners were well trained and so she held her hand out to Amy's mother.

"I'm glad that you could join us today," Mrs Haynes continued, "I understand that you live in London and don't know much of our country ways."

"No ma'am, but I have enjoyed myself picking potatoes," Emma flushed red as she forced the words out.

Not wanting to stress the girl out any more, Mary

155

Haynes gently patted her hand and began to move away. "Well, you are welcome to come up to the farm any time you wish while you are here."

"Thank you," smiled Emma and relaxed as Amy's mother went to collect the empty cups.

"Why do I get so nervous?!" she sighed to Amy and Becky.

"Because you're the complete opposite of me," replied Amy. "Believe me though, that isn't a bad thing. I'm often told I'm boisterous and brash and that it isn't becoming for a *young lady*!" Amy laughed out loud at the absurd idea of her being classed as a young lady.

"Speaking of boisterous and brash, here comes David," remarked Becky.

"Oh help," whispered Emma, desperately wishing she could blend into the background.

"*Lady Rebecca!* Lovely to see you and at last we get to meet your new friend. Hello. You're Emma aren't you? I'm David." He smiled and waved cheerily at her.

"H...H...Hello," Emma stammered.

Becky had noticed that Emma's nerves appeared worse when she spoke to boys and she couldn't help but raise a smile, surprised at how anyone could possibly find Amy's foolish, unassuming brother to be intimidating.

It was Amy who came to Emma's rescue.

"Don't you need to get back to your digging?" she

insisted. "Or we shall soon catch you up!"

"Okay. I know when I'm not wanted." He picked up his spade and made his way back across the field to where he had been working.

"Actually Amy, maybe you won't catch him up," said Becky. "If Emma is going to get washed, changed and back to the Coaching Inn before dark, we'll have to get going."

"Oh yes, of course. Just look at the state of me!" agreed Emma, holding her hands out in front of her and turning them over to see just how filthy they were. "Sorry that we can't stay any longer."

"That's alright. You've helped a lot today. I know Father will be grateful." Amy stepped forward and gave them both a hug. "See you soon."

"Yes," replied Emma. "And thank you. I've had a really wonderful afternoon."

5

"Hold on Amy," Becky called out of her bedroom window. "I'll be down in just a moment."

Amy was standing outside by the lock waiting impatiently. "Oh come on Becky. Hurry up!" she lamented.

Jim Bailey came around the side of the house. "Will you two quit shouting. There's enough noise coming from the town without your hollering at each other as well."

"Sorry Sir," Amy hurriedly apologised. She was a little scared of Becky's father and it was very rare that he spoke to her. Mindful of his hot temper she was eager not to anger him.

Becky's head remained at the window. "Are you coming with us to the fair Father?" Her voice sounded hopeful although in her head she already knew what the answer would be.

"Not likely," he snorted. "Just a bunch of yobs causing trouble, that's what the fair is."

"Okay, well I will be home in time to do dinner."

Becky knew better now than to argue. Once his mind was set he wouldn't be deterred. She picked up her bonnet and jacket and ran lightly down the stairs to join her friend outside.

"Goodbye Father."

He grunted a reply as they headed towards the town.

"What's wrong with him today?" asked Amy once they were across the lock and out of earshot.

"Oh, I don't know. He hates it when everyone goes off to the fair. Says the canal is too quiet. I don't know why he doesn't just join in."

It was the middle weekend in October. Most of the farmers had now finished their harvests and the town was celebrating its annual Michaelmas Fair. Michaelmas was the largest fair in the area. It was many times bigger than the Mayday attractions and drew visitors into the town from all over the area. On this special weekend the business and pleasure fairs all joined together to create one huge celebration. The stalls, tents and various amusements had been set up during the previous week and people were arriving in their thousands by coaches, carts, trains and on foot to be there. The sound of music, laughter and hundreds of chattering voices became gradually louder as the two girls walked along the side of the huge corn factory, making their way towards the bustling town centre.

"Is your money safe?" checked Amy as they were about to step around the corner.

"Yes," Becky patted her chest. Her purse was hanging around her neck, hidden under her clothes. She had spent many weeks saving so that she could enjoy all

159

the attractions at the fair and was well aware that unless kept safe there were doubtful characters around today who would swiftly relieve her of her savings if she wasn't careful.

The girls were not really interested in the livestock area of the fair which stretched from the marketplace right up through the streets, almost to the town hall. It was many times bigger than the weekly market which the town boasted. Stretching as far as the eye could see were horses, cattle, sheep and pigs, many of them rare, expensive breeds. Special carriages had been added to the trains to bring a large number of these animals in to the fair from around the country.

"I expect Father is enjoying himself in amongst that lot somewhere," said Amy. "Now, where are we meeting Emma?"

"Aunt Rosa said that they would be on the town hall steps at eleven o'clock."

They both looked up at the large clock, it was almost eleven now.

"I can't even see the steps, there are so many people everywhere. We'll have to go over there." Amy led the way as they fought and wriggled their way through the crowds to reach the town hall. Finding the steps, they looked up to see Aunt Rosa and Emma waiting for them. Standing beside Emma, looking uneasy and afraid, was Anne Cartwright. Emma spotted them emerging from the crowd and rushed forwards to greet them.

"Emma, No!" Miss Cartwright stepped forward and

sharply grabbed her back as though she were stepping in front of a train. "You mustn't rush off. It's dangerous here."

Amy looked at her bemused. She had heard a lot about Emma's governess and her fussy, high and mighty ways. Emma had told her friends that Anne Cartwright was in fact her mother's second cousin. Her father and mother had employed her as a favour to the family. Emma's mother did not have the heart to treat her strictly as 'staff' and as a result Miss Cartwright thought rather too much of herself. She even looked down on other servants and employees who were in reality her equal in status. This was the first occasion that Amy had met her.

"It's just a crowd of people. Emma is quite fine." Amy chose her words carefully so as to sound reassuring, however her tone betrayed her sarcasm. Anne Cartwright's eyes narrowed and she glared at Amy. Embarrassed, Becky nudged her sharply and stepped in front to politely address Emma, Aunt Rosa and the disapproving governess.

"Well where shall we go first?" she asked brightly. "The tombola maybe...?"

"I'm not altogether sure that this was a good idea," began Miss Cartwright.

Aunt Rosa quickly and calmly stepped in as Amy opened her mouth once again to rudely interrupt.

"Miss Cartwright, I can assure you that the girls will come to no harm at the fair. Today is a celebration for the town. They really will be fine, the three of them

161

together. However, if you would feel more comfortable at the Coaching Inn, I would be happy to escort you back. Today is one of the busiest days for the Inn and I must be getting back there now."

"But Mr Hamilton said that he would not be attending the fair because of '*its nature*'. How can I leave Emma here after he said that?"

"Mr Hamilton was referring to the hiring aspect of the fair. He prefers to hire his staff through more official means."

Miss Cartwright looked around her for a moment. "Well if that is really all there is to it, then, very good, I will return to the Inn with you Mrs Watkins. Emma dear, please take lots of care."

Aunt Rosa heaved a sigh of relief. She chose not to add that Mr Hamilton also disapproved of the heavy amounts of drinking and stealing that went on during Michaelmas. She had spoken truthfully enough; the girls would be fine, they would not be involved in *that* aspect of things so there was no need to mention it. She swiftly steered Miss Cartwright safely through the crowds and away from the fair before she could change her mind and spoil the girls' day.

Amy turned to Emma, laughing, "You weren't exaggerating about her! She looked like a frightened little rabbit."

Emma nodded, a little embarrassed.

"Amy, you really shouldn't be so rude to adults," admonished Becky. "You'll get into trouble one day."

"Oh, I know, I just couldn't help it," Amy replied, her eyes flashing mischievously. "I am sorry though. I shouldn't have teased her," she said, turning to Emma.

"It's okay," said Emma. "Anyway, let's forget Miss Cartwright. Are you two going to show me this wonderful fair that you've been getting so excited about or not?"

"Yes! Let's go," declared Amy, and linking arms, the three of them headed off towards the stalls and amusements of the pleasure fair.

Enthusiastically, they made their way from one stall to another, playing many of the different games that were set up for the crowd's amusement. They even had a ride on the big swinging boat that was set up outside the bakery.

"I hardly recognise anyone," noted Becky. Visitors had descended on the town from miles around.

"Just keep an eye on your money," warned Amy as a small, grubby child pulled at Emma's dress and held his hand out to ask for coins.

Emma nodded anxiously, looking apologetically at the young beggar.

"And don't be taken in by his sorrowful eyes. You can be sure his mother won't be far away keeping watch on how much he's collecting."

Before long the girls felt hungry and were drawn towards a food stall that smelt particularly good. They stood back for a few moments, choosing what to have.

"What do you think?" asked Amy.

"I don't really know what they sell, can we go closer and ask them?" Becky replied.

"Well, it says sausages from pig on the board."

Becky looked at her amazed. "Can you read that?! You've not had very many lessons!" she exclaimed, feeling slightly jealous at her friend's ability to read.

"Yes...well there are other words too, but I can't understand those."

"It says sausages from *German* pigs," added Emma.

"Oh, I see....*Geeerrrmaan.*" Amy read the word slowly to herself.

"Well, I can't read what it says so I'll just have whatever you two are having." Becky tried not to sound upset but it was hard to hide her envy of them both.

Amy knew how badly she wanted to learn to read. "Forget what else they have. Let's try the German pig. It sounds interesting... and looks popular," she added as a group of people came away from the stall with the hot sausages wrapped in paper in their hands.

They each ordered a sausage and a slice of bread then found a wall to sit on and enjoy their meal. As they were almost finished eating David came along.

"Ah, Amy, here you are. Yum, they smell good."

"They are!" said Amy, popping her last piece into her

mouth and grinning at him.

"The circus starts in a few minutes, are you girls coming?"

"Oh yes! Of course, the circus," cried Becky. "I'd forgotten about that. You'll love it Emma."

The circus was set up away from the stalls, inside a large tent. It was a popular attraction and they had to search to find four seats together. Sitting down, Becky looked around to see Mr and Mrs Hardy with Isabelle sitting not far from them. She waved to them and Isabelle stood on her chair and waved back furiously.

"She's a cute little girl," said Emma, watching Isabelle sit back down.

"Yes, she is," agreed Becky.

They enjoyed a good show. There were acrobats, clowns, ponies and even a giraffe. The girls cheered and clapped loudly as each act performed their tricks.

"So where are you girls heading now?" asked David, as they came out from the tent after the show was finished.

"It's probably about time for me to drop Emma back," said Becky.

It was now mid-afternoon and she was aware that some of the men at the fair had already been drinking for a few hours. From about this time onwards, it was inevitable that the tone of the fair would change from that of a happy celebration to a drunken brawl.

"Father and Mother were going to watch the three o'clock show in the theatre tent so they won't be ready to go home yet. Amy and I will walk up to the Coaching Inn with you," said David. "Besides, I wanted to see Joshua about something."

As they walked up Parsons Street towards the inn, Emma spoke. "I have a question." She was more comfortable in David's company now but her voice was still a little shaky. "I've seen many people walking around today carrying things like ladles, mops and even a few spades. It's most peculiar. Do you know why they're doing that?"

"That's because of the mop fair," David answered.

Emma still looked confused.

"It's to hire people," he explained. "They carry something to show their trade. The maids, for example, carry a mop. Then anyone who wants to hire a labourer or a servant will approach them to sort of interview them. If a job is offered and they accept then a ribbon is tied on them."

"Yes I saw the ribbons too," Emma said and then continued, "Is that what Uncle Joseph was talking about when he said that he prefers to hire officially."

"Yes, I think so," said Becky.

"Here we are," announced David, as they arrived at the Coaching Inn. "I'll just pop to the yard and see Joshua. Goodbye Emma."

The girls said goodbye and Emma went inside. Becky

and Amy found a tree to sit under and wait for David. They didn't have to wait long as David soon reappeared from the side of the inn.

"That was quick," said Amy, standing up.

"Joshua wasn't there."

"Really?" asked Becky, curiously. "That's strange; it's one of the busiest days of the year for the Inn. I can't imagine Mr Hamilton giving Joshua time off today."

"Never mind, I can see him another day. We'll walk back as far as the mill with you Becky."

David didn't tell her one of the other stable boys had told him that Joshua had left in a hurry to pull his father out of yet another drunken fight. He didn't want to spoil her day, although he suspected that she would hear about it before too long.

He carefully steered the two girls back through the town, purposely avoiding the area where the publicans had set up their tents for thirsty customers. David heard whistles of police constables and saw some commotion in the distance but cleverly diverted the girls' attention by pointing out to them some llamas that were being walked from the paddocks, where their menagerie had been on display, to a large coach and trailer which would transport them back to London.

When they got to the Flour Mill entrance the three of them parted ways. Amy and David made their way towards the cattle sheds to find Mr and Mrs Haynes while Becky slipped down the side of the factory to the

167

canal and the lockhouse, where her father would soon be expecting his evening meal.

6

The Coaching Inn had been bustling with guests arriving all day. Joshua had felt rushed off his feet rubbing horses down, stabling them and then cleaning the leather bridles and harnesses ready for the when the guests would leave the following day. The last thing he needed on this busy day was a problem with his father. When John Pickering had run into the yard asking him to go collect Tom Watkins from the fair, Joshua had at first been reluctant to leave the Inn. However, John had insisted that Joshua come down to the town and take his drunken father home.

Joshua followed John to a large tent that had been set up by one of the publican landlords.

"He was in there when I left, getting pretty mouthy. Was trying to start betting games with that fellow he had the argument with the other week. Mr Pennycad didn't want to cause a disturbance by throwing him out and so sent me to get you."

"Okay, thanks John. I'll just tell him he's needed back at the inn. He can fall asleep in the hay shed once I get him back. Hopefully Mr Hamilton won't realise that he hasn't been there working all day."

"Be careful Josh, he's been drinking *all* day," John

warned.

"Don't worry. I'm used to that."

Joshua was about to enter the tent when voices inside were suddenly raised and roaring and shouting could be heard.

"Sounds as though we're too late!" Joshua ran inside to see a chair being lifted above the heads of the crowd that was gathering in a circle in front of him.

He hurriedly pushed his way through to the front in time to see his father bring the wooden weapon down over another man's head and shoulders.

The intended victim wasn't really affected. He just stumbled a bit and then looked around for a suitable means of retaliation. But damage was definitely done elsewhere.

A farmer's son, who had been avidly watching a quiet game of dominoes before the fight started, was being swiftly ushered away from the commotion towards the exit of the tent by his father. The farmer thoughtlessly allowed his attention to veer towards the chair as it was lifted into the air giving the stupidly curious young lad an opportunity to sneak between the crowds to get a closer look. As Tom Watkins furiously brought the chair down upon his opponent a large splinter separated from it and flew through the air landing across the poor boy's head and cutting his scalp deeply.

With all the noise and excitement only a couple of people noticed him pass out and drop to the ground, blood flowing from the wound. It took a few moments for others to realise that the boy was injured. When Tom Watkins looked down and saw the damage he had done his face whitened and he anxiously looked around. His scared and wild eyes met with Joshua's for half a second before he pushed violently against the crowd and ran out of the tent and away into the town.

The next few moments passed by as blur to Joshua. He desperately wanted to rush after his father but he knew he should stay there, in the tent, to help the boy. The boy was being tended to and someone ran for the doctor.

Joshua just stood, frozen on the spot and stared in disbelief at everything around him. Would the boy be okay? The doctor wasn't sure. He needed to get him to his surgery and tend to him immediately. Police constables arrived and some spoke to witnesses. Others set out to find Tom Watkins. Mrs Pennycad brought a chair over and Joshua sat down, scared and frightened.

It seemed as though an age had passed. Eventually a message returned from the doctor's house; the boy would live but he was very badly injured. Where was Tom Watkins? Nobody knew, but he must be found. After a while, a constable approached Joshua. He wasn't from the town and had only come in to help look after the fair.

"Master Joshua Watkins?" he asked, sitting down beside him.

"Yes Sir?"

"We really need to find your father. Do you know where he may have gone?" he enquired.

Joshua thought quietly for a few moments. His mind was a blur, all he could think of was his mother and what she would say when he had to relay the awful scene to her.

"No Sir, I'm afraid I really don't know where he could be. Is he in a lot of trouble?"

"He hurt the boy very badly," the constable replied. "He will go to trial."

"And..." Joshua paused. "What then?"

The constable was an older man, his voice was gentle. He had questioned the witnesses enough to understand plenty of Tom Watkins violent, drunken character but also a little of his good natured, long-suffering wife and son.

"He most likely will get a sentence."

Joshua sighed.

The kindly constable continued, "However, it will be his first offence so I imagine it won't be as awful as it could be."

"I see."

Joshua knew that although it would be his father's first official offence, he had been given warnings numerous times in the past. This would not be of any help to him at the trial.

"Do you need to ask me anything?"

"No son, we have enough information." The constable patted him on the shoulder. "Why don't you head on back home and see your mother. I think the publican's wife has already gone ahead of you.

Joshua slowly made his way back to the Coaching Inn, dreading the look that he would see on his mother's face as he walked in through the door.

....

Tom Watkins was found before night fell, hiding in a shed by the railway. He was taken directly to Oxford gaol and put before a trial the following day. Found guilty of being drunk and disorderly and also causing bodily harm to a minor, he was sentenced to forty days hard labour during which time he would be kept under the supervision of the gaol. Most of the town commented that he should have received more punishment for the thing he did.

Aunt Rosa and Joshua knew that he was lucky not to be locked up for longer.

7

It was the end of a long day. The light outside was fading as Jim Bailey made his way indoors and took off his jacket and boots. He shivered to himself, the evening air was turning wintry. Becky had just got the fire in the front room going and was now busy preparing the meal. As her father sat back into his armchair someone rapped on the front door. He went to answer.

"Good evening Jim. Sorry to call so late but could Mr Hamilton and Mr Jenkins possibly have a brief word?"

Becky could hear Aunt Rosa's voice from where she was in the kitchen. Becky knew that Emma's father had returned from the north of the country a few days earlier but had no idea why they would be calling here with Aunt Rosa. She moved closer to the doorway so that she could clearly hear what was being said.

Jim Bailey, his usual self, greeted the two men without much enthusiasm and failed to invite them in.

"For goodness' sake Jim, it's not warm out here. Invite the gentlemen in," Aunt Rosa urged.

Becky heard her father grunt and then the three visitors stepped inside the house.

"It's a pleasure to meet you Mr Bailey," began Mr Jenkins. "I'd like to say what a wonderful daughter you have. She has done a great kindness looking after my Emma. I understand that they have become very close."

Aunt Rosa noticed that Jim Bailey's eyebrows first raised up sharply and then furrowed into a frown while the other man spoke.

"I have nothing to do with her gallivanting about town. What is it that she has done wrong?" Mr Bailey turned to yell for his daughter to come and join the conversation and explain whatever action the men were here to complain about.

Aunt Rosa quickly intercepted before he could call out for her. She placed her hand on his arm. "Jim, these men are here to *praise* Becky."

"Praise?!" he snorted. "Whatever for?"

Aunt Rosa sensed that the child was listening in the other room and her heart sank for her. "Just listen to what they have to say," she encouraged.

A little hesitantly now, unsure of what reaction to expect, Mr Jenkins continued, "As I was saying, your daughter and my Emma have become good friends. In a fortnight we are to return home to London and I would like to invite young Rebecca to accompany us for a few days."

Becky stood in the kitchen clutching onto a chair, barely able to draw breath.

"London?!" replied Jim Bailey. His voice was low and calm but the other man could see the confusion on his face. "Why ever would she want to go to London?"

"I thought that she would enjoy the time there with Emma and it would be our way of saying thank you for her help over the last few weeks," Mr Jenkins responded hopefully.

"I see no reason why she would want to go to London." Jim Bailey's tone clearly showed the scorn that he felt at this idea. "Besides," he continued, "it's out of the question. She is needed here."

Mr Hamilton now also joined in the conversation. "I understand Mr Bailey that your daughter looks after this little lockhouse and yourself very well indeed. She is to be commended. However, as she is still a young girl, do you not feel that she would enjoy a short trip away with her friend?" he spoke gently, softly. Aunt Rosa had pre-warned him that her brother-in-law was quick to take offence.

Mr Hamilton politely continued, "If you would permit young Rebecca to join my niece for a few days I would be more than happy for Rose to bring food from the Inn's kitchen to you each day as the young girl would obviously not be here to cook for you. Now, how would that sound to you Sir?"

Jim Bailey was suspicious. "But I don't understand why?"

"As Mr Jenkins said, Emma is very fond of your daughter and the family would like to show their gratitude for her friendship."

The lock keeper wasn't happy. He sighed deeply and

shifted his weight uncomfortably.

"How is Rebecca supposed to travel? I can't afford the fare to London," he asked, looking for a reason to decline this invitation that they were giving his daughter.

Aunt Rosa knew very well that he could pay for Becky to travel as a one off treat if he wanted to but she remained silent.

Mr Jenkins quickly provided him with the solution. "She will travel to London on the train with us as our guest. It is my understanding that a boat delivering timber to Mr Hardy is scheduled to leave London in a few weeks from now and the boatman is happy to bring Rebecca back if she helps out with the family and the journey."

Stood behind the doorway listening intently, everything was now clicking into place in Becky's mind. Earlier that day Mr Conway, a boatman for Mr Hardy, had gone through the lock with his family. He had winked cheekily at Becky as he had called out, 'see you *soon* young lady!' Now she understood what he had meant by the strange expression.

Jim Bailey paced fiercely around the small room in front of his visitors. He had been backed into a corner and he didn't like it that he had no other valid excuses to refuse their offer. There was one reason that immediately and rather surprisingly came to his mind but he was not going to tell them what it was. There was no way he could ever admit that this invitation had just brought it to his realisation that this child was his one and only precious link to his beloved wife, Myriam. He was shocked at the intense, deep concern he felt about sending her away. He was scared that sending her far away to a large and dangerous city would turn him crazy with worry. He had never realised before that he felt like this about her. No, he most certainly could not let them guess at the intense emotions he was feeling.

Finally he stopped pacing and stood still. "Then I suppose I shall have to let her go," he reluctantly agreed. "And, umm..." he tried to make his voice sound as casual as possible. "She'll be safe, I suppose...with you?

"Oh yes, very safe. You have no need to worry Mr Bailey," assured Mr Jenkins.

"Worry?! I wasn't worried. It's just the expected thing to ask," he derided. "Of course I won't worry. I'll be glad to have some peace," he muttered.

Aunt Rosa raised her eyebrows at him quizzically before asking, "May I go through and tell Becky the good news?"

"Do what you want," responded Jim Bailey, slumping back into his armchair with a deeply furrowed frown across his forehead.

"We'll wait in the carriage Rose," decided Mr Hamilton, unsure just how long the lock keeper's patience at their presence would last.

"Good evening Mr Bailey. Thank you for your time."

"Yes. Evening," Jim Bailey stared hard into the crackling fire, his mind trying to muddle through his peculiar thoughts.

Becky leapt at Aunt Rosa as she came into the kitchen.

"Oh Aunt Rosa, is it true? Am I really going to London?"

"Steady child, you'll have me over on the floor," Aunt Rosa laughed. "Yes, it's true. Aren't you a lucky, lucky girl?"

Becky jumped up and down joyfully and then slowly paused as a concerned expression came to her face.

"Is Father okay with this?"

Her voice was low so that her father would not hear from where he sat in the other room. Aunt Rosa glanced over her shoulder towards the room in which Jim Bailey was sitting.

"Yes, he'll be fine. I think he may even miss you." she whispered.

"Not likely," Becky shrugged. "He'll miss me cooking and cleaning for him."

"Well he'll have me to do that for him," Aunt Rosa said.

Becky still looked worried.

"What's the matter duckie, you do want to go don't you?"

179

"Yes, of course. It's just...aren't they rich? And well, I'm not."

"Becky let me tell you something. You, I, Emma, even dear Mr Hamilton, we have no idea what *rich* even looks like. Emma's family do have more money than you but I don't think they are *really* rich."

"They have a maid though."

"Yes, they have a maid. People who are *really* rich have *dozens* of maids and live in large, grand country estates."

Becky smiled. "Yes, that's true."

"Oh my dear Becky," Aunt Rosa held her close. "You'll have a wonderful time, you truly will."

8

The two weeks swiftly flew by and before Becky knew it, it was the day she was leaving for London. She had packed her bags early the night before, after carefully picking out her best dresses and cardigans to take with her.

She got up especially early to make sure that the little lockhouse was perfectly clean and tidy. After getting dressed Becky made her way down the stairway with her bag and coat. Fidget was lying curled up in her father's armchair. She gave him a long cuddle and wiped her tears on his fur as he purred loudly. "Be good and please stay out of Father's way," she pleaded with him as he settled back onto the warm cushion, blissfully unaware that she was going away and leaving him.

Her father had been in such an irritable mood the past few weeks since Mr Hamilton and Mr Jenkins had come to visit. Becky knew that he was annoyed that she was going away and she now felt nervous about saying goodbye to him. She made her way outside. Jim Bailey was over by the lock, looking up the canal.

"Goodbye Father."

Becky was standing close behind him. As he turned around to face her, she looked anxiously up at him, studying carefully his expression, trying to work out what he was thinking.

"I'll see you in a few weeks," she hesitated. He nodded, his mouth set hard and straight.

Becky wanted to hug him goodbye. She was sad to be leaving. She'd often seen other fathers hug their daughters goodbye. However, she couldn't remember him ever hugging her before and she didn't know how he would react if she were to put her arms around him. It might make him more annoyed with her. As she waited, he made no move towards her so Becky just turned around and crossed the lock.

"Bye," he feebly called out after her but she had disappeared around the corner and out of sight. He clenched his fists and beat them against his thighs feeling angry; angry that he'd not been able to say more to her, angry that he'd not been able to at least lift his hand to touch her gently on the head. She was gone now, it was too late and so he furiously opened the gate to the lock trying to block out the strange empty feeling that was coming over him.

Aunt Rosa and Joshua were waiting with Mr Jenkins, Emma and Miss Cartwright on the platform when Becky arrived at the station. Emma ran to meet her while Mr Jenkins took her bag. Miss Cartwright did not look impressed that Becky was going to be joining them but Becky was too excited to notice. Before long the train slowly pulled into the station and the doors to the carriages flew open as passengers began to alight.

"Well, we had better get on board," announced Mr Jenkins.

Becky turned to look at Aunt Rosa, her excitement mixed with feelings of sadness and apprehension. "I'll miss you!"

"Nonsense," replied Aunt Rosa, wiping a tear from her eye. "You'll be having too much fun to miss me. Here..." she handed her a small purse. "Get yourself something nice while you're away."

Becky gasped. "Oh thank you!" She hugged her tight. "I'll see you soon."

They got on the train and settled into a carriage. Mr Jenkins safely stowed the bags away and the two girls leaned out the window. The train let out a loud whistle and started to chug its way alongside the platform. Becky could feel the movement of the train as the wheels were turning.

"Oh my, its moving! Goodbye Aunt Rosa. Goodbye Josh."

She waved out the window until the smoke from the engine had covered the platform behind and she could no longer see them.

The engine picked up speed as it moved away from the station and Becky leaned out the window enjoying cool air rushing past her face. It wasn't long before her cheeks felt cold. Reluctantly, she was about to sit back inside and close the window when Emma exclaimed.

"Look!" Emma leaned forward and pointed out the

window. "Isn't that David and Amy?"

Indeed it was. They were standing in a field that ran alongside the rail tracks both waving ferociously at the train.

The girls waved madly back at them. Becky heaved a sigh of relief, delighted that Amy had trekked down through the fields to wave her goodbye. When Becky had first told her about Emma's invitation Amy had been extremely jealous and felt left out. However, Becky had patiently and kindly reassured her of her friendship. She was glad that her friend had got over her disappointment and had come to wave them goodbye.

Gradually, the train moved away from the view of the canal and river as it carried on through the countryside. Becky and Emma settled back into their seats after they closed the window to stop the cold November air from coming in. Mr Jenkins opened a book and Miss Cartwright closed her eyes, pretending to sleep while the girls chatted happily to each other pointing out different things as they passed them. The train stopped numerous times along the way, at Oxford and other smaller towns. It seemed to Becky that no time had passed before the green fields started to disappear, giving way to houses and buildings. The journey had gone so quickly, they were approaching London. As the houses got closer and closer together Becky again began to feel nervous. She sat up straight and peered warily out of the window while the train pulled into the large station at Marylebone.

Once the train had stopped, Mr Jenkins lifted down

the bags and Becky clutched anxiously onto hers as she stepped from the carriage onto one of the many platforms.

Emma was pleased to be back in London and comfortingly linked arms with her friend. "Come this way."

They followed Emma's father through the crowded and bustling station towards the exit. To Becky it was all so different from what she knew. Everyone was dressed smartly, carrying coats, umbrellas and smart cases. She glanced at her dress and neatly polished shoes, glad that she had chosen her best things to wear. Not a single person was wearing overalls or work boots here.

Outside there were horses and carriages and people everywhere.

"This way Becky, Father is getting a cab."

They made their way over to a black carriage and Miss Cartwright helped the girls inside while Mr Jenkins watched the driver secure the large cases that the three of them had travelled with. Becky kept her bag inside with her. When the cases were loaded Mr Jenkins also climbed inside and they set off towards Emma's home.

The roads were busy and there were shops and stalls and people everywhere. The wheels of the carriage bumped along the cobblestone roads. They passed rows and rows of houses that all looked the same to Becky. Soon they moved away from the busy part of the city towards the quieter suburbs. Passing street after street of houses Becky struggled to comprehend how so many people could live so close to each other.

Finally they turned into a quiet road with a long terrace of houses on each side. The carriage came to a stop outside number twenty-two.

"This is my home," announced Emma proudly.

Becky looked out. There were five steps leading up to the front door. It looked to her as though the house was three stories high, however there were steps also leading down below the pavement. Below road level there was a window looking out of what appeared to be a basement part of the house. It was completely different to her little cottage by the lock. She smiled back at Emma nervously. "It looks lovely."

"Mother will be waiting. Let's go in!"

Without waiting for the driver to get down and come around to the door, Emma had pushed the latch open and jumped down from the carriage and was running up the steps to her house. Tugging on the bell she cried out, "Mother, I'm home! Mother, it's me!"

As Mr Jenkins helped Becky down out of the cab, the front door to the house was opened by a lady wearing an apron.

"Hello Miss Cotton." Emma greeted the maid as she flew through the doorway to find her mother.

By the time Becky and the others reached the top of the steps, Emma had found her mother and they were both back at the front door to greet them.

"My goodness James, where is our Emma? Did you leave our quiet, timid daughter behind in the country?!"

Becky noticed that although Jane Jenkins was smiling and had a glint of laughter in her eyes it was obvious that she was an ill woman. Her complexion was pale and she was extremely thin. Her face looked tired and strained.

Mr Jenkins answered his wife with a kiss, "I told you that this trip had done her the world of good."

"Anne, it's lovely to see you." Mrs Jenkins gave Miss Cartwright a warm embrace. Looking over the governess' shoulders she smiled at Becky. "Hello dear. You must be Rebecca. I've heard much about you."

Her smile was kind and inviting. Becky felt her nerves dying away.

"Yes ma'am," she curtseyed. "I'm Becky. Thank you for having me."

Becky had been practising her greetings, anxious to be polite at all times.

"Now then, the air is cold out here. Let's get everyone inside." Mr Jenkins took his wife's arm and led everyone into the house.

They stood in the hallway and took off their coats. Becky was introduced to Miss Cotton who took their things from them and carried them upstairs.

"Becky, our house is your house. You must enjoy it as your own," instructed Mr Jenkins. "Downstairs is the

187

kitchen and Miss Cotton's room. The first floor is where you'll find our room, the study, Emma's room and Gwen's room and then Miss Cartwright is in the attic."

Becky looked around her. The hallway was nicely decorated and clean. She could see through to the sitting room with a large open fireplace. Aunt Rosa had been right; their house certainly was bigger than her small lock house but it wasn't overly grand. They weren't exceptionally rich.

Noticing her looking about Mrs Jenkins asked, "Is everything okay Becky?"

"Yes. I was just thinking how lovely and clean your home is."

Mr Jenkins had already informed his wife of Becky's situation at home, cleaning the house and looking after her father. She smiled. "Well, Miss Cotton does a good job tidying up after us all. Now would you like Emma to show you where you'll be sleeping or do you have any questions?"

"I do have one question?" Becky replied.

"Yes dear?"

"Who is Gwen?"

"Oh, Gwendoline. She is Emma's older sister. She is out at the moment, she is training to be a nurse. You will see her when she comes home later."

"Of course," Becky remembered that Emma had told her of her older, beautiful sister who was engaged and soon to be married.

"Come on, I'll show you my room," Emma took Becky's hand and led her upstairs.

Emma had a large room which looked out over the back garden. In the corner was a pull-out bed already made up for Becky. Emma opened the wardrobe which was full of beautiful dresses. She pushed some aside. "Here, you can hang your things in there. I hope you don't mind sharing with me."

"Of course not." Becky had never shared a room with anyone and she was quite excited by the idea.

"Come on, let's go and see if Miss Cotton has made afternoon tea and cake," said Emma and they made their way down to the kitchen.

....

Over the following few days Becky got used to life in London.

To begin with she woke early each morning, accustomed to rising early to start the work around the little lockhouse. After a few days however, she slept in for longer enjoying this new holiday routine.

Becky sat in on Emma's lessons each morning, much to the hidden disgust of Miss Cartwright. She learned to do simple adding and subtracting, to write the alphabet and to read a few basic words.

Becky met Snowball, the family's grossly overweight but very cuddly cat. She also met Gwen, Emma's glamorous older sister and her handsome fiancé.

Gwen was loud and outgoing, the complete opposite of Emma. Yet, she was kind to her younger sister and took the two girls out one afternoon to help her buy some lace for a dress that she was making. Becky enjoyed walking around the bustling streets. It was clear that Emma led a very indoor life in London. Her father worked in an office all day, her mother rested in her room and Miss Cartwright was not really interested in Emma once her lessons were finished. Most afternoons they stayed in Emma's room, playing games and drawing. It was a relief for Becky to step out into the fresh cold air and see something of London life outside of the Jenkinses' home. While Gwen picked out lace, Becky found a few gifts to take back to Banbury. She bought a scarf for Aunt Rosa, a little purse for Amy, some biscuits for David and a smart new cap for her father.

Each evening for dinner the whole family would sit at the table together. Becky admired the beautiful plates and fine cutlery and often popped down to the kitchen afterwards to enquire about how Miss Cotton had prepared the delicious meal.

In the evenings they would all sit playing cards together or listen to Emma while she played the piano for them. They were a close family and Becky enjoyed being a part of it.

Each night she would get into her warm pull-out bed and fall to sleep thinking of Amy, Aunt Rosa, Fidget and her father. They all seemed so far away from the quiet, calm city life that she was living.

9

Life in Banbury continued as normal for everyone except for Jim Bailey. He grumbled each morning as he cut his own bread and spread it with thick jam. He sighed and moaned to himself as he collected the eggs and fed the hens. He muttered despondently under his breath while raking out and re-laying the fire each evening. One thing that he didn't mind was the meal that Rosa brought down to him each day. Her cooking was good and having a belly full of warm tasty food lightened his mood for a few moments.

To begin with he had just grunted at Rosa when she arrived at his door with his dinner but as the days went by he found himself talking to her more, encouraging her to linger for a few minutes longer. Rosa knew that he would never admit to anyone that he missed his daughter's company but she could see it. She couldn't fail but notice the small glimmer of relief in his eyes when she said that she would step inside, just for five minutes.

Fidget found, much to his delight, that his presence too was becoming more tolerated as the days went by. Instead of being shooed out of the room, he was permitted to stay and lie in front of the warm fireplace while the man ate his meal. An occasional leftover was even passed in the cat's direction from time to time.

The evenings were long and quiet, too quiet. Jim Bailey found himself going up to bed earlier than usual each night, just to get away from the silence. Although the sounds he heard in his dreams weren't much better. He tossed and turned most of the night, unable to cope with Myriam's beautiful face and the sound of her voice talking to him as he tried to sleep. He was relieved when dawn would finally break, then he could go outside and get on with work.

It was a cold Friday afternoon, almost a week after Becky had gone and Jim Bailey had been working the lock all day without much rest. Fidget was scratching around in the log pile by the house. A barge approached from the south. Ron Hardy had been out for a walk and was now strolling alongside the heavy horse chatting to the boatman. Isabelle walked beside him, holding his hand. It was cold. Isabelle was wrapped up well in a smart little overcoat to keep her warm. Jim Bailey closed the gate as the boat came to a halt in the lock and walked to the other end of the lock to start letting the water in. He made his way back to where Mr Hardy and the boatman were standing waiting for the lock to fill up.

"Cat, Daddy. Cat!" Isabelle pointed over at Fidget.

"Yes, okay. You can play with the cat."

Isabelle ran over to the log pile and started to tickle Fidget while he jumped around.

The boatman was a regular through the town and the three men talked avidly about business. They were forced to raise their voices so that they could hear each other above the noise of the rushing water that was pouring into the lock and gradually lifting the boat higher.

"I must be getting on. Elizabeth will be wondering where we've got to," said Mr Hardy, turning to call for Isabelle.

"Where's she got to now?" he sighed.

Neither the little girl nor the cat were over by the log pile. The men looked around.

"Over there?" pointed the boatman.

Up the tow path, almost out of view they could see Fidget sitting on the pathway, his back to them, looking up the canal.

"She's getting far too independent! This is the second time this week that she has disappeared off without waiting for me," Ron Hardy lamented. "Now I'll be in trouble. She'll wander into the yard without me and Elizabeth will go mad that I've let her run off!" Mr Hardy ran off up the tow path in pursuit of his daughter.

Before long the lock was full and Jim Bailey opened the gate so that the boat could continue on its journey. The boatman nodded to another barge that was being lead past him down towards the lock. They stopped for a moment to passed the ropes over the other boat and the two horses squeezed past each other along the narrow tow path. By now it was late in the afternoon and Jim Bailey suspected that this could be the last boat for the day.

"Evening," he called. "Good timing, the lock is full. You'll be in and out in no time." He closed the gate and began to empty the lock.

Hearing hurried footsteps along the tow path he looked up to see Ben Coleman running down from the direction of the Hardys' yard.

"Mr Bailey, Isabelle isn't back at the yard. Mr Hardy sent me down to see if she's still round here somewhere. He said she was playing with your cat before he lost sight of her."

Mr Bailey looked up the tow path to see Fidget jumping out from the hedge in the distance. He frowned. "Well, the cat's up there messing about. Maybe she's climbed into the hedge and is playing hide and seek or something."

Ben went off to search the hedgerow while Jim Bailey got back to business. He shook his head and muttered to himself. He always thought that the Hardys fussed that girl too much. She was probably in the yard, hiding somewhere, thinking it was a great game. They worried too much if you asked his opinion.

The lock had almost finished emptying of water. The boatman was inside lighting the stove for his missus. Mr Bailey called to him that they could move on and he went down to open the bottom gate. The horse was led away and they continued on, aiming for Kings Sutton before it got too dark. Jim Bailey thought that they would be hard pushed to get there before nightfall. He picked up his lock key and started to pack up for the day.

He didn't know what it was that made him look over the edge into the lock. He never usually felt the need to check in there before going inside for the night but for some reason this evening he did.

He stood by the bottom gate and leaned over so that he could see down into the lock. Something he saw in there made his heart stop and the hairs on the back of his neck stand on end.

Floating in the water, resting against the corner of the open gate was a dark material. Jim Bailey knew instantly what it was. Shaking with fear, he ran for a rope, secured it and threw it into the lock. He climbed down as quickly as he could, almost slipping in, and grabbed hold of the navy overcoat.

Isabelle's body felt limp and heavy as he pulled it out of the freezing cold water. He held her under his arm, looking down at her briefly before climbing with difficulty back out of the lock. Although still hurrying to get her out of the lock he knew from what he had seen that she had already gone.

He reached the top of the lock and laid her out on the ground. Her wet hair clung to her blue lifeless face. He hopelessly blew into her mouth a few times to try and revive her but he knew that it was a pointless thing to do. It was too late. The water had completely filled her small lungs. He realized she had been in the lock for ages before he had found her. There was nothing that anyone could do.

He gently closed her eyelids to hide the scared, desperate eyes that stared up at him. Then, after picking her up carefully, as one would a new born baby, he began the agonizing walk that he knew he had to make towards the Hardys' yard.

Jim Bailey did not make it to the Hardys' house. The relief that came over him when he realized he wouldn't have to face Elizabeth filled him with feelings of guilt. He had not walked far when he met with Ron Hardy who was coming back along the tow path, anxiously retracing his steps. The light was very low by now but Jim Bailey could see enough to recognise the anguish on the other man's face as he caught sight of the lock keeper walking heavily towards him carrying a tiny burden, laid out across his arms. Jim's heart sank lower as Ron's cry pierced the evening air and he fell hard to his knees, unable to look at the sight in front of him.

Breathing in deeply, Jim Bailey brought the man's poor child to him and supported his friend while his tears poured out, his head bent over his daughter's cold body.

It seemed as though an age had passed before the two men stood up and parted ways. One carrying his beloved baby home to his poor dear wife; the other to go back and face the scene of what had happened.

Feeling numb, Jim Bailey walked past the lock and on into the house. He sat down in the armchair without lighting the lantern or the fire and remained there in silence.

Then from nowhere the floodgates opened and, for the first time in his life, Jim Bailey cried his heart out. He cried for the little girl that had laid lifeless in his arms. He cried for the years he had lost being unable to connect with his own beautiful daughter. Above all, his tears flowed, at long last, for the loss of his precious wife, Myriam.

10

"Which do you think looks best?"

"The pink one I suppose," replied Emma dismally.

"Yes, the pink one looks lovely!" Becky was more enthusiastic.

They were in Gwen's room, sitting on the edge of her bed, both watching while she pinned her hair up elegantly on her head and then secured a simple pink flower to her curls, adding to the beauty of her careful arrangement.

"You look like a princess!" exclaimed Becky.

"It's so unfair that we can't go down for the dance too," moaned Emma.

Gwen turned around to look at the two girls; one frowning and pouting, the other inquisitive and mesmerised by the beautiful new dress that she was wearing.

"Come on Emma, don't be silly. You know that this is a special grown up party for Mother. Don't spoil the evening for your friend by sulking."

Mr and Mrs Jenkins were holding an evening party for all their friends. Emma's mother had been sick and away from everyone for many months and now that she was almost fully recovered and feeling a lot stronger they wanted to celebrate. They were putting on a small buffet and dance at their home but Emma and Becky were not permitted to attend. For Becky it was exciting enough to just see decorations going up, musicians arriving and the adults in the family rushing around and getting themselves dressed up in beautiful clothes. However, for Emma this was all she ever got to see. It just didn't seem fair that she and her friend couldn't join in the occasion.

"Besides," Gwen added. "What would you do if you were invited? Just hide in the corner like a scared goose?"

Emma's eyes filled with tears and she ran to her own bedroom across the hall. Becky remained there, standing awkwardly, not knowing what to do.

"Oh dear," sighed Gwen. "I shouldn't have teased her. Becky, would you mind putting my powder and lip liner into the purse for me while I go and apologise?"

Becky walked over to the large dresser that stood by the window. She put the powder and lip liner carefully into the dainty cream coloured purse. Catching sight of herself in the mirror she held the purse gently under her arm and curtseyed. "Good evening Miss Bailey." She greeted her own reflection.

"Pleased to meet you Miss."

Becky's eyes widened as she noticed that Mr Jenkins was standing behind her. Flushing pink, she spun around to face him.

He smiled. "Next time you come to visit we will have a party just for you and Emma."

"Do you promise Father, really?!" Emma came rushing back into the room having heard her father's words.

"Yes, I do," he patted her gently on the head. "Now listen you two. Miss Cotton has made some special treats for your supper and you'll be able to see a lot of the dancing from the top of the stairs."

Becky was elated. She looked expectantly at her friend.

Emma paused, still upset that they weren't allowed downstairs. She saw Becky's excited face and decided not to make any more fuss. "That sounds great father! Thank you." She hugged her father and Becky grinned eagerly at them both.

"Well don't you think you should both go and get dressed and do your hair?"

They looked at him, confused.

"In case anyone should look up and see you both peeking through the banisters," he explained.

"Yes, of course! Come on Becky," Emma grabbed her hand and dragged her off to her bedroom so that they could get themselves ready for the *show* they were about to watch.

Minutes later the girls were sitting at the top of the stairs, in their best dresses, holding plates piled high with fancy finger food from the buffet, watching as the guests arrived for the party.

Emma's mother, although looking pale and drained, stood in the entrance hall dressed in a beautiful sparkling gown and greeted her friends one by one. Her husband stood beside her, gently supporting her frail frame, his warm smile welcoming everyone into their home.

The small quartet of musicians were playing soft tuneful music in the large drawing room, which had been cleared of all furniture for the occasion. Gradually, they increased the tempo of the music to encourage everyone to start dancing.

Emma and Becky sat transfixed, eagerly watching the dresses swishing and swaying as the gentlemen led the ladies around the room. Becky was enchanted. Everyone moved so perfectly in time with the music. To her they looked like flowers dancing happily in the wind. At the end of each song the dancers would applaud, partners would change and then they would begin again.

Before long the little band played a song which Emma recognised.

"Oh, I know this one!" she gasped. "Come on, I'll teach you."

She grabbed Becky's hand, forcing her to stand up.

"I'll be the gentleman, you just follow my lead."

The two girls curtseyed and bowed to one another and then spun each other around the landing laughing happily to themselves.

"You see, we didn't need to go downstairs to enjoy the party," giggled Becky, accidentally standing on Emma's feet for the third time.

"No, we didn't," Emma agreed.

It didn't take long for Becky to pick up the steps and she was delighted to finally be learning to dance as she had always dreamed of doing.

The evening continued late into the night and once they were worn out dancing around they sat back down on the stairs determined not to miss a thing. As their eyes grew heavy, and they fought desperately to stay awake, the music slowed down and the guests began to head home. After the last guest had gone, Mr Jenkins carried his tired wife up the stairs to find the two girls laid stretched out across the landing, fast asleep.

"If I had enough strength, I would carry all three of you," he chuckled and carefully stepped over them to put his wife gently into bed.

11

The time in London seemed to fly by and before Becky knew it her ten days with Emma's family were over and it was time for her to head back home to Banbury.

Becky was sad to leave. She had enjoyed being part of this happy, peaceful family. She preferred the cheerful evenings they had all spent together in the sitting room talking or playing games to her silent, lonely evenings in the lockhouse. She had experienced the fun of living with others her own age, having a play friend and someone to giggle with all day. Most of all she had appreciated living in a house with a maid and so not having to cook and clean for her father.

Becky packed her small bag and took one last look around Emma's room before carefully placing a small envelope on the little dressing table. She had softened Miss Cartwright with a jar of sweets bought from a shop in town so that she would help her to write a simple 'thank you' card. It was short but for Becky it was one of her biggest achievements academically. The sketch on the front was of a man and woman dancing. She had also bought the card during her trip into town. Inside it read;

Dear Mr and Mrs Jenkins, Gwendoline and Emma,
Thank you very much for my stay in London.
I have loved it.

With love
Becky

Becky carried her bag downstairs. Emma and her father were waiting by the front door to take her to the docks where she was going to the meet the Conway family to travel back along the canal with them. Becky had already said goodbye to Gwen after breakfast. However, Mrs Jenkins was not feeling well, as she had not slept well, so Becky was not able to say goodbye to her before leaving.

Mr Jenkins had fetched a cab and it was waiting for them outside.

"It's quite cold outside, I think you will both need your coats and gloves," he told the two girls.

The driver was pacing up and down along the pavement trying to keep warm. His horse was waiting patiently. As they came outside he ran to the side of the black cab, opened the door and helped them in.

The journey to the docks seemed longer than the journey they had taken from the train station when Becky had first arrived. Becky didn't know which of the two was closer, but she did know that this journey today was not nearly as exciting as the other had been. They didn't talk much while riding inside the carriage. Mr Jenkins was reading the morning paper and the two girls sat silently holding hands. Each too sad to say something, afraid they might cry.

They arrived at the busy Regent Canal Dockyard and the cab stopped amid great carts and carriages loading and unloading all sorts of different cargo. To Becky it looked busier here than the train station had been when they had arrived in London. They jumped out from the carriage and Mr Jenkins instructed them to follow him closely while he tried to locate the barge on which the Conways were travelling. Finally after much wandering around they found the registration numbers and name of their boat, 'Water View'. Mrs Conway had painted a few roses and castles along the outside of the cabin, as had many other boat owners. Emma was pleased to see that the boat looked welcoming for her friend.

"Where are the family?" she asked Becky, looking around.

At that moment a small boy, aged about nine years old, wearing a tatty jacket with a red handkerchief tied around his neck came out from the cabin.

"Hi, Becky. Pa said I had to look out for you."

"Tommy. Hello," Becky replied. "Where are your ma and pa?"

"Pa's doin' the papers an' getting' the toll fares, Ma's gone to get some bread an' meat. I've gotta tie the old tarpaulin over the timber. Wanna help?"

"I'm sorry Becky but I'm afraid we'll have to go," interrupted Mr Jenkins. "I asked the cab to wait but I don't think he'll hold on for too long. Are you okay if we leave you now?"

"Of course." She was secretly relieved. Emma had said that morning that she wanted to see inside the cabin of a boat. But Becky didn't want her friend to see just how tight and confined her journey home was going to be. It was better that they had to go now.

The two girls turned to face each other. Both blinking back the tears that were threatening to escape from their eyes.

"I'll miss you," said Emma, giving her a hug.

"Me too," sniffed Becky.

"Father has promised we can come to Banbury again soon."

"I can't wait."

And that was it. Emma quickly turned to walk back to the waiting carriage before the tears fell. Mr Jenkins also gave Becky a quick hug and then they had disappeared into the crowds.

Becky wiped her eyes and followed young Tommy up to the hull of the boat which was already loaded with timber, ready for the journey to Banbury. She climbed around and helped him to stretch out and fasten the tarpaulin securely over the cargo so that it would not get damaged during the trip. While doing so Becky looked down at the marks and dirt that were already on her dress and congratulated herself that she had packed her best dresses safely away in the bottom of her bag.

Before long Mrs Conway returned. Her grey coat was stained with coal and other grime. She had long, dark hair which had been plaited down her back and then wound up into a tight bun on top of her head. She walked carrying a basket on one arm, full of provisions for the next few days. On the other arm was a baby, about ten months old.

"Ah, Becky, you found us alright. Good. Pa wanted to get goin' as soon as we could. Here, take Maisie while I get this all inside."

Mrs Conway passed the grubby little baby to Becky. Becky sat on a block and bounced her up and down on her knee.

"Great, everyone's here. Let's hitch up quickly an' go. I wanna get through to Kensington today."

Mr Conway smiled at Becky with a friendly glint in his eye. He was leading a medium sized, dark-bay draught pony alongside him.

"Tommy, watch the load, while Ma steers. I'll lead Ruby through here, else she'll spook. Becky, you stay inside the cabin with the baby. Send Ma out to help us. I'll show you what to do out here when we're away from the docks."

Becky picked up her bag while still balancing little Maisie in her arms and stepped onto the boat before climbing down into the cabin.

"I've just warmed her some milk. Keep the stove goin', coals are out there, in the box."

Mrs Conway, disappeared out through the hatch doors and Becky put her bag down on the bench before letting out a sigh.

It wasn't a sad sigh. It was more of a realisation that

she was back to reality. Becky knew that her journey home had been negotiated with the intention of her helping out with all the jobs, however after a week of pleasing herself it was a hard thing to accept. Sitting on the small bench at the side of the cabin, she looked around at the tiny living space she was in. Opposite her was a small stove with a shelf behind and a cupboard to the side. The door to the cupboard was hinged to drop down as a table for preparing food and eating. Past there was another bench which would be turned into Mr and Mrs Conway's bed at night. There were two small cupboards above and Becky could see that one had been set up as a small cot for Maisie. The bench that Becky was sitting on also doubled as a small bed and Becky guessed that Tommy and herself would be sleeping top and tail in there each night.

Maisie started to grumble so Becky pushed her bag to the corner of the bench out of everyone's way, and reached for the bottle of milk. Maisie sucked away happily at the warm milk while Becky watched out the small window as they moved slowly out of the busy dockyard and up Regent's Canal. This was the heart of London's industry. There were boats and barges of all shapes and sizes moored up, loading and unloading. Cogs and pulleys were lifting even the heaviest loads from off the water and placing them on the ground.

They seemed to have got away earlier than most and made good progress along the busy canal. Before long Maisie had fallen to sleep so Becky placed her gently into the specially adapted cupboard and then fetched a few more coals for the stove. She boiled some water and made a hot drink to take out for Mr and Mrs Conway. Mrs Conway was steering and Mr Conway was walking beside Ruby.

"See Ma, she's a good girl this one, I knew she'd be no trouble." He took the hot mug gratefully. "So Becky, you've never been this far down the canal?"

"No." Becky shook her head.

"Well, it may be a slightly longer route the way I'm going but it will be interesting for you."

Becky knew that Mr Conway refused to go on the part of the Thames that went right through the middle of the city. He had lost three horses in the last two years because they had drowned in the river. The traffic that went along that wide section of river was bigger and bulkier than the usual canal traffic. The twists and turns of the natural river made it awkward to pass others along the tow path. And the currents could run strong. He'd never lost a horse in a canal and so Mr Conway had decided that for the sake of an extra night or two travelling he'd rather travel along the Regent's Canal to the Grand Junction and then join the Thames further up where it was calmer and quieter. He couldn't afford to risk losing any more horses. Good, strong horses weren't cheap.

Becky also knew that what Mr Conway had said was true, it would be more interesting going along this section of canal. She had heard about the long tunnels on this part of the waterways and the famous steam tug that was at Islington and she was excited to see it.

"Here, I've finished with that," he said, handing the mug back to her. "Just get back on the boat while we pass this one."

It seemed like they were passing people every few minutes. There were so many more boats on the move here than up on the sleepy backwater of the Oxford canal. Each time they passed someone it required careful steering and advance preparation. They needed to slow the pace, which meant looking ahead as there was no quick way to stop a moving boat. Then the rope had to be lengthened between the horse and the boat so that it could sink to the bottom of the canal. Mrs Conway would carefully then steer the boat towards the opposite bank so that the oncoming boat could pass over the top of their sunken rope. Any mistakes or lack of concentration could result in impact with the other boat or, worse still, a horse losing its footing.

Mr and Mrs Conway had a perfected, well practised driving routine along this busy stretch and so Becky went back inside the cabin to watch Maisie.

It wasn't long before they were at the Islington tunnel and joined the line of boats waiting to be pulled through by the steam powered tug. Ruby was unhitched and Tommy held her while Mr Conway tied the '*Water View*' securely to the boat in front.

Mrs Conway came into the cabin, her fingers blue from the cold.

"I must find my gloves," she shivered.

Becky was eagerly looking out the window.

"You can go an' sit on the timber with Tommy an' watch if you want," she said. "I wanna make some lunch so I'll watch Maisie. You'll need to wrap up mind, it's bitter cold out there."

Becky pulled her gloves on and climbed out to join Tommy where he was sitting on top of the tarpaulin. She watched as the steam tug was linked up to the boat at the front of the line. They were third in a line of four that were going to be pulled through the tunnel. The tug was able to pull a few boats at the same time. Once they were all hitched up the steam tug started to move, aided by a long chain that ran below them. With a small jolt the whole line was moving. The powerful little tug was pulling them along the canal like a little train on water. As they went into the tunnel the light faded and inside it was dark and damp. The tug ahead had a lantern on board and from its dim light Becky could just make out that the tunnel roof was not far above their heads. If she were to stand up she would hit it. They could hear the chug of the steam engine and quickly Becky reached for her handkerchief as the steam blew back to her mouth. Tommy did the same and they sat in silence breathing through the cotton so as not to choke on the smoke. Before long they could see daylight getting brighter and they came out the other side. A couple of boats were already lined up waiting to go through where they had come from. Mr Conway had walked Ruby over the top of the tunnel and was waiting to hitch her back up. She had a nose bag on and was happily eating some feed while they got everything ready to go again. Mrs Conway came out with some ham sandwiches which Mr Conway ate while fixing Ruby back up to the boat.

"Your lunch is inside, Becky," said Mrs Conway. "It's another busy stretch now so I'll 'ave to be out here, I need you to watch Maisie again for me."

"Thank you." Becky smiled, it was cold outside so she didn't mind too much sitting inside the little cabin.

Before long, Maisie was grumbling again. She started by just screwing her face up and letting out little groans. Becky gave her a tour of the tiny cabin, pointing out anything that looked remotely interesting. She would smile for a minute before again screwing up her face and starting to cry. Becky would then quickly move to another point of interest. This only lasted so long before little Maisie realised that they were looking at the same things over and over. Her groans became more persistent and her cries got louder. Soon she was screaming and there was nothing Becky could do to quieten her. She tried giving her a biscuit to suck on but Maisie just threw it to the ground in a temper while continuing to wail out loud. Becky's head began to ache. As she patted her, trying desperately to console her, Becky felt that the little baby's bottom was a bit damp. She realised that a foul odour she thought had been coming from outside was in reality coming from the baby's nappy.

Becky opened the hatch. "I think Maisie has messed her nappy," she called to Mrs Conway.

"You'll need to change her then. Her things are in the corner of her little bed."

Becky didn't find Mrs Conway disapproving like Miss Cartwright had been but she was very direct and cold in her manner. Becky felt no warmth from the woman and sighed as she closed the hatched and was again trapped with the screams and smells that were coming from the little baby.

Becky reached up into the cupboard to find a sponge and some clean nappy cloths. She had watched a long time ago as Mrs Hardy had changed tiny Isabelle when she was a baby and Becky tried her best to remember what to do. After pouring some warm water from the kettle into a bowl, she laid Maisie down on the bench and took off the soiled nappy. Becky had to hold her breath as she disposed of the soiled section and threw the dirty cloth into a pan of boiling water on the stove. She then carefully wiped the baby's bottom clean and wrapped her up in a clean nappy cloth securing it with a pin. She sat Maisie back up and to her dismay the little girl was still crying.

 Mrs Conway leaned in the hatch. "She may want some more warm milk. There's a can of it hanging from the boat."

Becky climbed out through the hatch, passed Mrs Conway her child and carefully made her way along the boat to where several lengths of rope were hanging various cans in the water to keep the contents cool. The first can she lifted out contained drinking water, the second had a block of cheese inside. The third can she lifted out was full of milk. Becky took the lid off, poured some into a mug, replaced the lid and carefully lowered the can back into the water.

Taking Maisie back into her arms she climbed down inside the cabin again and warmed the milk before giving it to the small, sobbing baby. It worked. The screams stopped and she even started smiling. Becky finished washing the dirty nappy cloth and hung it over the stove to dry.

By this time they had arrived at Eyre's Tunnel. Although still a long tunnel compared to anything Becky had seen before, this was the smallest of the tunnels on the Regent's Canal and there was no tug here. There were however leggers; men who would 'leg' the boats through the tunnel for you for a small fee. Mr Conway again unhitched Ruby. This time he asked Becky if she'd like to lead Ruby over the tunnel while the boat was expertly legged through. Tommy walked with Becky as she led Ruby along the trail that went over the tunnel and then back down to the tow path. It was hard work for the legger and they waited for a few moments for the boat to appear.

Ruby was again hitched up and they continued on as before.

It was late afternoon when they arrived at Maida Hill, the last tunnel. Mr Conway had wanted to clear all the tunnels on the first day. He spoke to a legger, eager to go home before night fell. Mr Conway convinced him that if he helped him to leg the boat through it would be quicker. The man agreed and again Becky and Tommy led Ruby over the tunnel. This was a longer tunnel and they waited a long time for the two men to leg the boat through. Becky had left her gloves inside the cabin and so warmed her hands in Ruby's thick coat.

It was almost dark as Ruby was hitched up for the last time and they carried on towards Kensington Docks. Mr Conway had a few extra bits of timber to collect for

Mr Hardy there and he wanted to be there overnight so they could load and be away at first light the next day.

Alone in the cabin as they travelled the last few miles to the dock, Becky started to cut up and cook some potatoes and sausages that Mrs Conway had bought that morning for dinner.

When they arrived at Kensington the boat was moored securely. Ruby was brushed and led to a stable to enjoy a feed and a rest. Then the family came inside to find that the meal was ready. Becky noticed Mrs Conway smile.

Mr Conway's eyes glinted as he looked at his wife and said, "See Ma, as I said before...she's no trouble at all."

ONE FINE LADY

Winter

1

Jim Bailey shuddered as he sat down cautiously on the cold, hard wooden pew and looked anxiously around him. He let out a deep sigh and watched as the vapours from his breath rose up in front of his tired, strained face. It was always cold inside a church, but today it was bitterly cold outside also. He could remember with vivid clarity the last time he had sat inside St Mary's, even though it had been over a decade ago. It had been a scorching hot summer's day when they had buried his dear Myriam and yet the inside of the church had felt much the same as it did now. Maybe people felt that if the building were freezing then the memories of the deceased would be preserved for longer, he reasoned to himself, trying to calm the beats that that were pounding furiously from his heart. Jim Bailey had sworn to never again enter into the building where he had been forced to say farewell to his beautiful wife all those years ago. He had successfully kept that personal promise all those years; that is until now. All morning he had battled with his emotions and his conscience as to whether to attend the funeral service of little Isabelle Hardy or not. Finally, his broken heart had given way to his humane head and after he had dressed in a suitable pair of black trousers along with a blazer, he had apprehensively made his way through the town to the church.

Many from the town were arriving and taking their seats inside the large building. Some were lamenting the early onset of cold weather while others were sitting respectfully, allowing their thoughts to be with poor Mr and Mrs Hardy who were both seated quietly down the front. Pale and gaunt they looked as if they had not slept a wink since the terrible accident five days earlier.

The coffin arrived and the service began. The minister was doing his best to comfort the grieving parents but Jim Bailey felt there were no words that could ease their pain. No happy memory that could replace that feeling of loss. No future promise that could halt their present tears. He closed his ears to it all and tried to think of other things. Yet, hard as he tried, thoughts of her lifeless little body, floating in the lock, kept haunting him. His knuckles were white as he gripped tightly onto the pew in front of him. He didn't know how much more he could take.

The congregation was standing to sing the hymn now. He stood also but with no hymn sheet in his hand. He felt numb and empty. He needed to focus on happier times. With hesitation he undid the mental lock that he had placed upon himself all those years ago and cautiously began to allow his mind to wander to thoughts of Myriam. He remembered their courtship and then their happy wedding day. In his mind's eye he could see her raking over the garden behind the lockhouse. She looked up from a row of carrots she was planting and smiled at him, he smiled back.

He was beginning to feel calmer, his heart had stopped racing as it had been all morning.

Then he could see her pregnant, her hands cradling her bump. She was happy.

'Here Jim, I can feel the baby kicking!' she called from his memory. 'He's got a good kick.'

Jim Bailey's tight grip was now released from the pew and he was feeling more relaxed.

'It might be girl!' he laughed.

She nodded back. 'That would be lovely.'

Myriam had always wanted the baby to be a girl.

Then, as his memory reminded him, the labour started and her beautiful, happy face changed. It was so painful, too painful really. He knew that something wasn't right. The doctor was fussing and Myriam was so pale, so ill.

Inside the church they were saying a prayer over the small body that lay within the coffin. Inside Jim Bailey's head however, his memories were unloading out of control. He was trying to soothe the crying baby while comforting his sickly wife. The baby took up so much time; feeding, changing and washing. Myriam was getting weaker as the months went by. He couldn't give his attention to both of them. The child was walking now, opening all the cupboards and drawers, getting under his feet. And then, without warning, his mind brought him to that awful, final day. The day he had shut out of his thoughts for so long.

As the minister's final words sounded through the

church, Jim Bailey pressed his hands hard against his head, but he couldn't make it stop. Myriam was there, lying in his arms. Her life was slowing fading. He was reaching out to her, stroking her but he wasn't able to pull her back to him.

The congregation murmured in unison, "Amen," and that was it; Myriam was gone.

Jim Bailey was now gasping for air. He pushed through the crowds and ran straight outside into the freezing air. He coughed and spluttered, trying to catch his breath. Aunt Rosa had been watching him carefully during the service and now she made her way over and threw her shawl over his shoulders. He jumped in surprise and stared at her, his scared eyes red with grief.

"Let's get you home duck," she said, and gently began to lead him to the lockhouse.

2

Becky lay in the small bunk staring up at the panels above her. She had just spent her first night on the canal boat. Outside it was beginning to get light but she had been lying awake for ages. Sighing, she turned her head to the side and glanced at the pair of feet beside her. The feet that had kicked her sharply in the head numerous times over the previous eight hours. The cold, clammy feet that belonged to young Tommy Conway. Becky and Tommy had shared the bed each sleeping at opposite ends, toe to head. The young boy had wriggled and kicked around all night long. Becky had pushed herself as close to the side of the boat as she could but he had just enjoyed having more room to move about. She felt as though she had hardly slept at all.

She could hear Maisie gently gurgling to herself as she lay in the cupboard which had been especially adapted for her to sleep safely in. Becky had not heard a sound from the small baby all night. She had slept peacefully, like an angel. Becky wished she were small enough to share the tiny cupboard with the little baby instead of this lively youngster who was now puffing breaths of cold air onto her own feet.

She could hear movement from behind the curtain where Mr and Mrs Conway had been sleeping. They were starting to tidy their bed away. Each morning the beds all needed to be packed away to make room for the family to move about within the small living space.

Becky reached up to the shelf where she had laid her clothes out the night before. The air was very cold, much colder than she had expected it to be. Uncomfortably aware of her changing body and a little embarrassed to be sharing a bed with the younger boy, Becky was eager to dress as quickly as possible before Tommy should wake up and the Conways would finish getting themselves ready. Still half under the blankets, protecting her privacy, she pulled her vest over her head and tights onto her legs. Struggling to pull her dress straight she got out of the bunk and stood on the cold wooden floor.

"Gracious, I need to find my shoes quickly!" she shivered under her breath.

Mrs Conway had heard her. "Is that you child? It's like an in ice cave in here. Get the stove goin' will you?"

Becky opened the door to the stove. The embers had died down but there was still warmth in them. She poked around and added some fresh lumps of coal. Before long it was heating up. Mr Conway pulled back the curtain and greeted Becky cheerfully.

"You're a good un' kid. It's mighty cold today hey? They said it was comin', this cold weather, but I didn't think it would be this early in the year. I'll open up the hatch and fill the can for us. Can you get some water boiling, I could do with a quick wash."

Becky started the water boiling and then filled a nose

bag with some food and took it down to Ruby while the family had a quick wash. She would wash later once they were all finished.

Ruby was stabled just a few yards away. Becky stood with her hands under Ruby's thick mane while the horse ate her breakfast. Becky loved watching horses. They were such big, gentle giants. Ruby's big eyelashes blinked now and then and her huge stomach gurgled as she crunched and munched on the oats and carrots which Becky had given her.

Mr Conway came up to pay the stabling fees and get Ruby ready for towing. "You can head back down to the boat now Becky, Ma's just puttin' some food on for us."

Back at the boat Becky slipped behind the curtain and had a quick wash with the remaining warm water. Then she sliced the bread and got some plates out for the family while Mrs Conway cooked a pan full of eggs. They all ate quickly and then packed everything away ready to get going again on the canal. A few boats were already moving and Mr Conway was anxious to get started as well. It was so busy on the canal around London and there were so many boats to pass all the time that if you didn't start early then you wouldn't cover many miles before the day was finished.

"I need to sort little Maisie out, why don't you help outside?" suggested Mrs Conway.

Becky wrapped up warm in her coat and hat and pulled her gloves firmly onto her hands. She pleased to go outside and help. She had spent a lot of time inside the boat yesterday. Mr Conway showed her the best way to lead Ruby and helped her to pass other boats when they came to them. Tommy, now awake, washed and dressed, was steering the boat carefully so as not to hit the bank of the canal or any other boats. For a young boy Becky thought he concentrated well on his job.

The canal was busy but it felt quieter than it had the previous day. There were no tunnels to navigate through and only a few locks and bridges. If they hadn't passed so many other boats they would have probably made it all the way to the Grand Junction. As it was, they moored up in the Yeading Dock that night.

Becky had been outside leading Ruby all day. Mrs Conway had taken the opportunity to get on with some washing and sewing inside the boat. Items of clothing were hanging above the stove drying. When they had secured the boat and brushed and fed Ruby, Mr Conway, Becky and Tommy made their way into the small living space. Becky felt chilled to her bones. Walking alongside Ruby all day had kept her from freezing too much but the cold seemed to have set right inside her. She huddled next to the stove, wrapped in a blanket.

Mrs Conway let out a sigh, about to make a remark that the girl was in her way. Mr Conway perceived this and quickly intercepted his wife's thoughts.

"The children both did well today ma'," he commented, pushing an also shivering Tommy towards the warm stove.

"Aye?" she replied.

"You wouldn't believe how cold it is out!" he continued, "I'd swear it were the middle o' January if I didn't know any better. Folks 're sayin' we're in for a terrible winter. These two 'ave done well out there today. Let 'em warm a bit hey?"

He smiled gently at them both and Mrs Conway's frown disappeared.

"Well, while you're sat there Tommy, make yerself useful an' stir that broth will you." She sat down and waited patiently while Becky and Tommy warmed up enough to move back from the stove and sit on the bench.

The winter evening was long inside a small canal boat. Five people in such a small space could get on top of each other. Becky occupied Maisie while Tommy played a game with his father. Mrs Conway finished her sewing. Eventually it was time for them to make up the beds. Becky felt exhausted and she slept well, unconscious of the kicking, fidgeting boy beside her.

The next day they made it to the Grand Junction and then followed the River Brent for a few miles before reaching the Thames. Heading west along the river Becky noticed immediately how much quieter it was now than it had been in London. There were no big factories and as they left the city the tow path became more like the country path she was used to walking along at home. She did find it odd being on a river though. The canal was so straight and direct in comparison to the natural twists and turns of a river.

As the days went by Becky felt that they were flying along and she would be home in no time. She was glad. Although extremely grateful to the Conway family for allowing her to travel with them, she was not used to being confined with so many people like this. Becky lived a very solitary life back home and sharing a tiny space with four other people was hard for her.

She also longed to be back at home because for some reason she felt unusually tearful. Becky was never a girl for unnecessary tears but just now she seemed to be either irritated or saddened by most things. Little did she realize that this was all part of the complicated changes that were going on with her body but no one had really explained any of this to her, so she went through each day confused at the way she was feeling which worsened her sadness. Mrs Conway didn't seem to notice the dejected look on Becky's face and Becky felt that poor Maisie would have a hard time as she grew up with this woman as her mother.

Now they were away from the city, each night they had to stop and attempt to find either stables or a friendly farmer they could pay to accommodate Ruby for the night. In summer she could be tethered to some nearby grass but it was far too cold to leave her out at night. When stables weren't nearby it was often difficult to find a willing farmer. Many of the boatmen and their families were not reputable and sadly the farmers along the canals and other waterways were the ones who lost out to their thieving.

Walking across the fields to request a stable they would have to carry a broom and spade as farm dogs would sometimes be let loose to chase them off. Mr Conway often felt disheartened that he was lumped in with a bad bunch. He tried hard to be honest and respectable but many others had already given him the bad name of being a 'water gypsy'.

Becky received this same stigma when accompanying Mrs Conway into the small towns to buy provisions. Mrs Conway dressed in simple clothes, thick warm boots with her hair tied up on the back of her head looked every bit a boatman's wife and the women in the towns treated her as such. They watched suspiciously while she made her way around their store, putting items into a small basket. They counted her coins carefully to see whether she had indeed given them the correct amount. Becky felt sad for this kind family who were as honest as she had ever met. She felt that it wasn't fair.

Only eight days after leaving the first dock in London they reached the Oxford Canal. Mr Conway was pleased with their progress considering there were only a few hours of daylight at this time of year. While in Oxford Mr Conway had a farrier put some new shoes on Ruby and he bought a set of new ropes. The ropes wore down quickly from constant wear through the water and along the bridges. While Mr Conway was taking care of these things Mrs Conway took Tommy to the shops to fill the boat up with enough food until they would reach Banbury in two or three days' time. Becky remained in the boat with Maisie and carefully polished Ruby's thick leather harnesses.

She hadn't been polishing for long when she heard a lot of commotion coming from outside the boat.

Looking out of the small window Becky could see there was heavy splashing in the water and people were running around in panic. Becky picked Maisie up, wrapped her in a blanket and hurried outside to see what was happening.

A poor horse had slipped on the ice and had fallen into the water. The animal was thrashing around, with rope and harness all still attached, trying to get out. Becky shuddered to think how cold the icy water must feel to the frightened animal. The hauler was shouting earnestly for help while trying to calm the fear stricken beast.

Becky stared helplessly as men rushed to find planks of wood. The Conway's always carried a strong plank on top of their boat in case of accidents such as this.

Becky yelled out, "Here! We have a plank over here."

A man came running over and grabbed the long plank of wood from the boat. The men placed the planks they had gathered into the canal to make a ramp for the horse to walk up. But the terrified creature did not understand that this was his way out to safety. He continued scrabbling at the steep bank beside the planks. The hauler was now at his wits end. Securing a rope around his own waist and handing the end to the biggest man he could see, he bravely made his way down the ramp into the canal. His body tensed and he hesitated a little as the freezing water began to swirl around him, but he knew he must continue if he was to save his horse. The horse was getting tired now and his attempts at the bank were slower. The man swam over to the animal, talking softly all the time.

229

Miraculously the petrified horse took notice of his voice and stopped kicking around long enough for the man to reach out and take hold of his harness. Calling the horse he pulled him gently and swam back to the makeshift ramp, leading the horse with him.

Desperately throwing the rope from the horse's harness onto the bank for others to catch, the hauler pulled himself quickly out of the water to avoid the strong, deadly legs of the horse which were now scrambling to get a grip on the slippery ramp. The men stood on the side of the canal, heaved and pulled the cold, wet horse up the ramp to safety and threw blankets over him. The hauler, now also freezing and tired from his exertions was pulled out of the water and taken somewhere warm to recover.

Becky's pulse, which had been racing, returned to normal and she sighed in relief. Then she shivered. Realising she had covered Maisie with a blanket but had forgotten to grab a coat for herself, Becky quickly made her way back into the boat to warm up.

3

Aunt Rosa's steps were deliberate and slow as she carefully made her way along the wooden gate of the lock. She held her breath. It was dark. In one hand she held her lamp and in the other a basket of food for her brother-in-law. The ground was slippery and she could feel that the lock's gate was icy beneath her. She must not lose her footing now, not while she walked ten feet above the deathly cold canal water, along a narrow piece of timber. Reaching the other side, she breathed in deeply. The cold air hit her lungs and she coughed a little.

"Rose, is that you?" Jim Bailey had heard her and had come to the door.

"Yes duckie. Here, take this basket."

She handed him the large wicker basket and followed him indoors. The fire was going and she stood warming her hands against the flames.

"Gracious, look at this huge chunk of ham," Jim Bailey called from the pantry where he was unpacking the basket. "Thank you."

Aunt Rosa smirked to herself. It was odd to hear him speak with enthusiasm and gratitude. Yet, this was not the first time recently that he had spoken to her in this courteous way.

....

After the funeral she had accompanied him home and they had sat silently together inside the small lockhouse for almost an hour. Eventually, Aunt Rosa had judged it to be the right moment to speak.

"You know, it's alright to grieve dear," she had assured him.

He looked at her and nodded sorrowfully, his eyes sadder than she had ever seen them. Aunt Rosa did notice though that some of the tension from his forehead appeared to have gone.

"It's also okay to remember," she continued.

He nodded again and opened his mouth to speak.

"I've pushed her out of my thoughts all these years Rose, thinking that it was the best thing to do. I've hidden myself from each reminder, each memory, each emotion. I've been trapped in a prison for so long, unable to live as I should. Unable to reach anyone on the outside. Unable to let anyone in."

Aunt Rosa nodded in agreement. They were both thinking of Becky. Poor, innocent little Becky had spent years knocking on the door to her father's emotional cell.

"Today, whilst sitting inside that church it all broke out. I faced it, but it was scary."

"I know, I know," she reassured him.

"What do I do now?" he looked at her intently. "How

do I work this mess out?"

He had grabbed her hands and was pleading with her to help him.

Her heart went out to him. She looked into his wide, frightened eyes. Gently she explained that he needed to continue to think of Myriam; both the happy times and the sad. He needed to grieve for her, no matter how hard he may find it at times. This was the only way he could find freedom from the heavy cloud of fear that had been with him since she had gone.

"And then, you need to show that child that you love her," she said softly but firmly.

"How?"

"Well, I can't tell you that. That's something you need to do by yourself."

He looked back at her desperately.

"Believe me," she continued, "if you allow yourself to really cherish the memory of dear, sweet Myriam, you'll know just how to love your precious, little girl.

....

He had followed the advice she had given him and it was working. As Jim Bailey allowed himself to remember and even to talk about his beloved wife he felt lighter and freer. It was as though a great burden had been taken away from him. People commented on the changes they were seeing. The frown lines were less visible, he held real conversations and he even seemed to smile a little. Harsh, abrupt orders were gradually being replaced with kind, appreciative words.

Aunt Rosa, enjoyed hearing his gratitude. He had always been happy and grateful to everyone before Myriam had died. The Jim Bailey she had known as a young woman was kind and caring, even carefree. But this fierce, angry stranger had overtaken him during the past ten years and she had forgotten the way things had used to be. It made her happy to see the real man returning now.

He came in from the kitchen and sat down in his armchair. Fidget came and pushed himself around his feet, purring. Aunt Rosa smiled; even the cat could sense a change in this man.

"Have you any idea when Becky will be home?" she asked.

"No. I had a telegram today saying that they left London a week ago, on the same day as little Isabelle's funeral. They should only be a day or two away now, I imagine."

"I wonder if the cold weather has slowed the journey at all," she commented.

"Well, I know that Timothy Conway only uses the canals in London, so that will add at least a day to the journey. But they should move quickly once they get out of the city. Most use the Grand Union now. The Thames and our canal will be quiet." He paused. "Mind you, if we get bad ice, they could be a long time. I don't think they run many icebreakers down here anymore. Sent them all to the Grand Union I think. If they're not near one of them and a big freeze comes, we won't see them for a long while."

He looked sad.

"You missing her duckie?" she asked gently.

"I just want to know she's safe," he replied. "It seems like she's been gone for ages."

Aunt Rosa could hardly believe what she was hearing. Three weeks ago he'd barely even looked at the child as she had tried to hug him goodbye and now here he was, counting down the days until she returned. Aunt Rosa wasn't sure how Becky would react to this change in her father. One thing was certain; the girl was in for a shock!

"I know," she said comfortingly, patting his hand. "She won't be long now."

4

It took longer than Mr Conway had expected to get things sorted and it was well after midday before they moved away from Oxford. There had been a lot of commotion after the horse had slipped into the canal which had caused a bit of a queue for boats coming in and going out of the area. Eventually they made their way up the canal but the light was already getting low in the cold wintry sky. They only progressed a few miles past Oxford before it became too dark to continue safely.

They stopped on the outskirts of the small hamlet of Yarnton and after securing the boat Mr Conway lead Ruby off to find some suitable stabling for the night. It seemed an age had passed before he returned, walking wearily along the tow path. They had been looking out for him and saw the glow from his oil lamp swinging with each stride.

"That's odd," commented Mrs Conway. "I'm sure I can hear the sound o' horse's hooves with him."

Sure enough Mr Conway had returned with Ruby.

"Pa, what happened, is there no space for the mare?" she asked.

"Oh, I'm sure there be space enough," he sighed. "Just none for the likes of our mare. Seems our hard working Ruby ain't good enough to be welcomed 'ere.

"But why not Mr Conway?" asked Becky.

"Cos we're 'water gypsies' an' our mare might steal somethin' from their farm in the night!"

"For goodness sake!" cried Mrs Conway. "Do they not feel the cold out 'ere?" She looked at her husband in disbelief. "What'll we do?"

"We've got no choice but to tether her 'ere by the boat," he replied. "We'll 'ave to cover her with some good thick blankets and take it in turns every hour to walk her round a bit, not that she'll like that much, but we'll need to keep her warm.

It was a long cold night for them all. Ruby was tied securely a short distance from the boat along a grass verge. She had a big nose bag of feed and they covered her with four large blankets. As the night continued they took it in turns to go out with the lamp and walk her around the outside of the field that they were moored by. Tommy and Becky went together, too scared to go out into the dark night alone. Shivering together under their own blankets they jogged, almost running, around the field with the sleepy Ruby trotting along behind, stumbling in the shadows. Neither the humans inside the boat nor the bewildered horse outside got much sleep that night.

When daylight eventually broke through the black sky, they awoke to find the situation had become worse. Mr Conway pulled his clothes on, and slipped out of bed, trying not to disturb anyone else in the boat. As he tied his boot laces he could see the breath from his mouth rising up into the air like smoke from a pipe. He wrapped a scarf around his neck while quietly cursing the farmers from the tiny hamlet.

"Fancy not giving a stable for a poor horse when it's as cold as this," he muttered to himself.

Filling the nosebag, he took it out to Ruby. She nuzzled against him and he stroked her under the blankets. She felt warm at least. He was relieved.

His breath was puffing out as short blasts of steam from his nostrils, he turned and looked up the canal. The water appeared smooth and translucent in the pale morning light. The surface of the canal was still, not a single ripple. It was like looking at a large pane of glass. Everything was so peaceful. Too peaceful he thought to himself. Mr Conway made his way to the water's edge. He picked up a small stone from the tow path and threw it out in front of him. He knew before the stone landed what was going to happen, he'd done it before, on mornings just as bitter as this one. The stone hit the shiny surface of the canal and instead of splashing into the water and sending gentle ripples out to the other side, it bounced three times before skating across the ice and stopping a short distance from the opposite bank.

Ice; the water had frozen overnight to form a layer of ice. He shrugged. It was still the beginning of December. It wouldn't be a thick layer of ice. They had nothing to worry about, the boat would break it up easily, he reasoned to himself. He turned and was about to go back to the boat, but instead looked around for a larger, heavier stone. He wanted to make be sure how thick the ice was. Under the hedge he found one, it was more like a rock. Perfect. He lifted it above his head and with a surge of effort he flung it down onto the canal. It landed and chipped the ice a tiny bit sending one small crack out across the surface but it didn't disappear as he had thought it would. Astounded he stared at the rock as it lay on top of the ice.

Nervously he glanced up and down the canal. There was no one else moored within sight. Other boatmen must have made it to proper moorings at Tackley or back in Oxford.

Mr Conway awakened the family quickly and harnessed Ruby to the boat. Tommy and Becky emerged from the cabin bleary eyed from the nights activities.

"We need to work as a team today," he instructed them.

They nodded at him sleepily.

"Becky you lead Ruby, see if you can get 'er to pull really hard. Tommy, we won't need you to steer, we won't be movin' fast enough. Take this shovel to the front of the boat an' help me dig at the ice."

Becky and Tommy were soon alert. They sensed the urgency in Mr Conway's voice and knew they had to help as much as they could.

Mr Conway and Tommy swung and drove their tools into the ice while perched on the side of the boat. Bit by bit they broke up chunks of ice but the progress was painfully slow. Mr Conway decided to tie his young son around the waist with a rope and secure it to the boat as, more than once, the weight of his swinging shovel nearly carried him over into the icy water. Becky piled the blankets back on top of Ruby as they weren't moving fast enough to keep the poor horse warm. Exhausted they stopped for lunch and a hot drink.

"Where's the beastly icebreakers when you need them?!" lamented Mrs Conway.

"On the Grand Union I expect," replied Mr Conway.

"There must be some 'ere somewhere."

"Aye, there'll be some," he assured her. "But they could be miles away."

The Oxford canal was becoming little used now in comparison with the Grand Union. Services required by the boatmen, such as the specially designed icebreaker boats, were not now readily available. Mr Conway knew they would need to continue digging themselves through the ice if they wanted to make any progress at all.

As the day went on, the air warmed up a little and the ice became easier to break up. They felt as if they made a lot more progress during the afternoon than they had in the morning. Still, by the end of the afternoon they had only covered a few short miles since setting off that morning. Then, just moments before dusk, they saw another boat coming towards them.

"Of all the bad luck," moaned Mrs Conway.

Becky didn't understand.

"They've broken up the ice as they've come towards us," Mr Conway explained.

Becky still didn't understand why that wasn't a good thing.

"Well, if we'd 'ave met them earlier it would've been great," he said. "We could 'ave travelled quickly through the water behind them. But it's almost dark now so we'll need to stop here anyway."

It seemed that luck really wasn't on their side at all on this day. Mr Conway had encountered this boatman and his family before and they really were 'water gypsies'. He didn't trust them one bit. He wasn't going to let Ruby out of his sight with them moored right beside them. After lighting a small fire close to where the horse was tethered and wrapping up in coats and blankets he laid out on the cold ground and resigned himself to what would probably be the most uncomfortable night of his life.

5

The progress along the canal remained slow for Becky and the Conway Family. Each night the water refroze and they again had to spend the day painfully beating away at the frozen canal in order to advance any further on their journey.

By the third day they were out of meat, flour and milk. Mr Conway set off to some nearby woods to try and trap a rabbit or two while Becky was sent to search for someone who would sell them a few things, or at least give them something edible in exchange for a few lumps of coal. She nervously approached a small farm not far from the canal and held her breath as the farmer's wife came out to see what she wanted. To her relief they were friendly and happily traded the coal for flour and sold her two cans of milk. Amazingly, they also agreed to rent them a stable and so Ruby enjoyed a warm, dry bed for the night. To Mr Conway's delight he was also successful and managed to snare two rabbits. So they all rested easy that evening.

On the fourth day they were delighted to pass the icebreaker and to their amazement covered twelve miles before darkness fell. They had made it to Heyford Wharf; now only a day's journey from home.

Awakening the next morning, Becky realized how excited she was to be almost home. It had been difficult sharing this small space with the Conway family for the past two weeks. She felt constantly cold and weak from working outside all day in the winter air. She was eager to see Amy and Aunt Rosa. She couldn't wait to warm her face against Fidget's thick fur and to stretch out in her own comfortable bed. And, although it surprised her because she hadn't expected it, she was looking forward to seeing her father.

She got dressed early and began preparing breakfast for the family. She packed her things carefully in her bag, ready to take it off the boat with her when they would arrive in Banbury later.

Cloud had covered the sky overnight and so the air temperature had risen slightly. There was a thin layer of ice on the surface of the canal but nothing that they couldn't easily break up with their own boat as Ruby pulled it through the water. Compared to the slow progress over the last few days it felt like they were moving quickly. As they covered each mile, they got closer and closer to Banbury.

They stopped briefly for lunch at Aynho Wharf and Becky was now really excited. Only a few more hours and she would be home. She was leading Ruby along with Mr Conway when they came towards the arch bridge. Banbury was only a mile away now. Becky looked up the hill towards Amy's farm. She had an idea.

"Mr Conway, would it be a terrible bother if I left you here?" she asked.

"Not a problem for us. We've got to get used to not 'avin you with us tomorrow anyway, so no reason why we can't continue on our own now," he replied. "But... aren't you eager to get home?" he added.

"Well, yes..." she hesitated. "It's just my friend Amy lives up the hill there and I thought I might see her quickly. I have a gift for her you see."

"Right enough, you carry on. We'll tell your father that you're following on behind."

"Thank you. And thank you so much for allowing me to travel with you. It's been ever so kind of you all."

Mrs Conway looked out of the hatch to say goodbye but they weren't the type for sentiments so Becky thanked them again and made her way up the hill towards the farm. She chuckled to herself; this would be such a surprise for Amy.

She crossed the farmyard and knocked on the door to the kitchen at the side of the house. After a few moments she heard footsteps coming. Mrs Haynes, wearing an apron and covered in flour, opened the door.

"Gracious, it's Becky. You're back from London!"

Becky heard a scream from upstairs and the thud of Amy rushing down the stairs to greet her.

"Oh yay, you're back. I missed you, I really did!" Amy threw her arms around her friend's neck and jumped up and down shaking poor Becky to pieces.

"And you've grown. I'm sure you have," Amy

exclaimed.

Becky laughed. "I've missed you too."

"Well, come in out of the cold, and stop letting all our warmth outside," urged Mrs Haynes.

Becky stepped inside. Amy took her bag and she looked nervously around at her mother before she asked Becky, "Haven't you been home yet?"

Becky was hanging her coat on the hook by the door and something in Amy's tone made her turn and face them both. "No. I jumped off the boat as it passed by your fields. Why, is something wrong?" she asked cautiously.

"Humm…" Amy paused.

"Nothing wrong at all duckie, just your father will be wondering where you are."

Stepping forwards to pull out a chair for Becky to sit down, Mrs Haynes swiftly interrupted her daughter.

"Come on, that's hardly true. He wouldn't bother if I was back today or next week," Becky shrugged and sat down.

Mrs Haynes placed a cup of tea and a slice of cake in front of her. "From what I hear he's been looking out for you for a few days now."

Becky had taken a sip of her tea. She slowly placed the cup back onto its saucer and looked them both straight in the eyes. Amy looked away, avoiding her gaze. Mrs Haynes' eyes appeared gentle, even more so than usual, a hint of a tear almost. They were both hiding something from her.

Becky felt nervous. "Father never looks out for me. What makes you think he is now?"

Mrs Haynes leant across the table and took Becky's hands into hers. She spoke softly. "A terrible accident happened here just after you left for London," she paused, trying to find the right words to say. "Dear little Isabelle Hardy fell into the lock."

Becky gasped. "But she's okay, isn't she?"

Mrs Haynes slowly shook her head.

"Did she drown?"

Mrs Haynes nodded. Becky's eyes filled with tears. Her face screwed up as she started to cry.

"Oh no, poor Isabelle. Poor little Isabelle."

Amy came around the table and hugged her friend. After a few moments Becky rubbed her eyes and looked up again at Mrs Haynes. "Are Mr and Mrs Hardy okay?"

"Well we haven't seen them but I've heard they are struggling," she replied. "Becky," she continued. "It was your father who found her, in the lock."

"Probably best," she replied. "Father's used to that, he's seen many accidents over the years. It would have been awful if Mr or Mrs Hardy had found her."

"Becky, your father may have seen many accidents but

I think this one was different."

"Folks are saying your father's taken it worse than anyone," said Amy.

Becky frowned. "Really?"

"Yes."

"And Becky..." repeated Mrs Haynes. "Folks say he really has been looking out for you."

"Well, I very much doubt it, but there won't be daylight for much longer so I should start heading home anyway."

She tried to sound cheerful as she put her coat on, her eyes still red from crying.

"I'll soon get to see Fidget." Becky struggled to perk up. "Oh, I almost forgot, I got you a gift Amy. And I didn't ask you, how is school?"

Amy felt subdued. "Oh, it's fine, I can read quite well now."

Amy politely admired her new purse and Becky left the biscuits for David as he was outside somewhere with his father.

They said a quiet goodbye and Becky made her way down the hill towards the canal. It hadn't been the happy homecoming reunion that she had hoped for.

Walking the along the tow path towards the town she couldn't steer her thoughts away from little Isabelle. Becky looked down at the water and the image of the innocent little girl haunted her. By the time she arrived in the town her mood was very low. She turned her thoughts to Fidget to try and lighten her spirits. It was almost dark as she approached the lock yet there were plenty of people moving around as it was still only mid-afternoon. Although some of the lanterns around the lock had been lit, Becky couldn't make out who was who in the distance and she supposed her father must be ahead of her somewhere, fiddling with the lock gate or across with Mr Dickenson in the coal shed.

Focusing on what she was approaching up ahead around the lock she hadn't noticed that someone had been stood still, down on the tow path. It wasn't until she almost walked into them that she noticed they were there.

"Rebecca, is that you?"

It was a man's voice, his tone was anxious.

"Father?"

"Oh, thank goodness, it is you."

He took a step towards her. Becky stopped still in her tracks. She couldn't believe it; he had been looking out for her after all.

In the dim light he approached and stopped just in front of her. His breathing was fast, yet concentrated as though he was consciously trying to calm it down. His arms were by his sides, fists slightly clenched but not in his usual agitated way. He had a look in his eyes that she had never seen before. It was a vulnerable, strained look. Becky would never know but he had anxiously been standing in that spot for over an hour, waiting for her to return safely along the tow path.

Slowly he reached out his arms towards her. For a moment Becky felt sure he was going the pull her close to him and hug her.

She held her breath.

He also held his.

Then with his right arm he took her bag, and his left, he closed around over her shoulder giving her a gentle squeeze. It wasn't the warm embrace that he knew he should have given her but it was the best he could do.

Becky could feel his arm shaking around her. She felt shaky herself. She knew she had to follow his lead and not push beyond the affection he was now showing. She smiled at him.

"I missed you Father."

She felt him let out a deep sigh. Then he did something she'd never seen him do before; gently and deliberately he looked down at her and smiled back.

"I'm glad you're home."

They walked together silently to the lockhouse; The father walking along with his arm around his daughter. Unseen by the pair, Mr Dickenson was smiling as he peeped through the cracks in the door of his coal shed. Then Fidget joined them. He purred and rubbed happily around their legs as they made their way inside.

Becky's heart felt warm inside. It wasn't at all like the silent, unresponsive homecoming she had been expecting. It had been a hundred times better.

6

It was late before they went to sleep that night. They sat in the front room together, talking. As the time went by Becky discreetly kept pinching herself as she couldn't believe what was happening. For the first time in years they were having a real conversation. He listened carefully as she told him all about Emma's family and their house and of all the things she had seen in London. He tried on his new cap and said that he liked it. He even asked a few questions, wanting to hear her talk more.

He warmed up some food that Aunt Rosa had brought by the previous evening and they sat in front of the fire eating together. Becky had not yet set foot in the kitchen. He asked her about the journey home, and how it had been travelling along the canal. The conversation slowed as Becky exhausted all her stories. She then asked him a few questions about what he had been eating and how things were with Fidget and Aunt Rosa. He was not as talkative as she had been but his answers were not as short and curt as she was used to. Then, after a while the room fell silent. The only sound was a gentle roar from Fidget as he purred contentedly, now lying in front of the warm fire.

Becky looked at her father while he sat and stared at the dancing flames. Should she mention Isabelle's name? Would he tell her about what had happened that day? She thought about it. No, she decided. It would be best not to ask. She stood up and made her way towards the kitchen and the stairway.

"Goodnight Father," she said.

"Goodnight," he replied.

The next morning after breakfast Becky set off to visit Aunt Rosa. She popped the scarf in a little bag and set off towards the town. Jim Bailey watched anxiously while she walked across the slippery wooden gate.

Mr Dickenson noticed his concern. "It's lovely to see young Becky back from her journey Jim."

Jim Bailey nodded and smiled at his old friend.

Becky arrived at the Coaching Inn and made her way to the kitchens. She knocked the door, turned the handle and walked in. Aunt Rosa turned around from the stove to see who it was. She threw her wooden spoon high into the air and let out a loud shriek. "Ahhh, it's you! Dear Becky, you're back. Come in, come in!"

Becky shut the door behind her.

"Sit down child. Wait there. I need to stir this sauce for five more minutes."

Becky sat down at the large kitchen table. She found it amusing to watch Aunt Rosa as she excitedly stirred the white sauce she was making while turning every few seconds to flash Becky a cheeky grin. Some of the kitchen girls were working around the kitchen and they said hello to Becky. Before long the sauce was done. She poured it over a pan of cooked vegetables and popped it into the oven before coming over to join Becky where she was sitting.

Becky stood up to greet her properly and Aunt Rosa pulled her in and held her tight for what felt like forever.

"Ah I have missed you duckie. It felt like you were away for years!   Now stand back and let me have a good look at you."

Becky stood back and Aunt Rosa stared in admiration at her niece. Clasping her hands together with emotion she exclaimed. "I do believe you've grown child. And look at how you've fixed your hair, so elegant. Is that the way they all have it in London? You look like a proper little lady!"

Becky laughed at her Aunt's enthusiasm. "Oh Aunt Rosa, I have missed you."

"Well, I want to hear all about it. Come, I'll make a cup of tea and you can tell me everything, right from the beginning."

So Becky told her all about her time away. Aunt Rosa listened avidly to her tales of the carriage rides, the busy streets, the party at Emma's home and the long icy journey home.

"Yes," commented Aunt Rosa when Becky had finished telling her about the horse that had fallen in the canal. "We were beginning to worry that the journey was taking you all so long." She paused. "Your father especially."

253

Becky looked her directly in the eyes. "Father's different, Aunt Rosa. It's very odd...but in a good way," she added.

Aunt Rosa's mouth twitched the start of a smile.

"I think he was looking out for me when I arrived home last night," Becky continued, "can you believe it?! Actually standing on the tow path waiting for me! And he put his arm on my shoulders...Aunt Rosa he almost hugged me!"

"As I said, we were all worried that your journey was taking so long."

"Come on Aunt Rosa, he's not behaving the same as normal. We sat together and talked last night, and I mean really *talked*. Like you and I are talking now!"

Aunt Rosa patted her gently on the hand.

"I know. He's been talking to me too."

Aunt Rosa put her hand to her head and anxiously touched her hair. Becky could tell she was nervous about what she wanted to say. Reading her thoughts Becky spoke first.

"The Hayneses told me about Isabelle's accident."

Aunt Rosa looked relieved that she already knew.

Becky continued, "They said that father found her."

"Yes love, he did."

"What happened?"

Aunt Rosa shook her head. "Nobody can say for sure. She was playing, with Fidget, and the men were talking. A boat was in the lock. When dear Ron Hardy looked around they couldn't see the girl anywhere. All they could see was Fidget, up the tow path towards the Hardys' yard. They assumed she'd got bored and wandered home. But of course she hadn't and it was your father who later found her little body in the lock and had to take her down to them."

Becky was again crying.

"Do you think that has something to do with the way Father is now?"

"Most certainly I do." She took a breath and continued, "Becky, your father went to the funeral, in St Mary's church.

Becky stared at her. "No, he never would have gone in there?"

"He did, although it was so hard for him. I could see him from where I was sitting the entire time. He was white as a bed sheet. The moment the service ended he rushed out of the church and I followed him. He was in a panic, he had faced a fear and it had really shaken him."

"Poor Father."

"But that was the moment that touched him Becky. I think that while he was struggling inside that church, he realised just how important you are to him."

Becky looked at her confused.

"But I'm not important to father."

"Of course you are child."

"He's never cared about me."

"He's *always* cared about you," Aunt Rosa insisted. "He just never knew he cared until a few weeks ago."

"Maybe that's right. But what if he forgets to care again tomorrow? What happens then?"

Becky looked sad, worried that this change in her father's feelings would only be short lived.

Aunt Rosa nodded. "I understand your fears duckie. I really do. I've got a good feeling about this though. Trust me."

Becky shrugged. "We'll see."

She realised she hadn't heard any of Aunt Rosa's news. "Anyway, how are you? Is Uncle Tom back yet?"

"I'm just fine," she replied. "I've had a peaceful few weeks. And yes...your uncle is back."

"Is he okay?" she asked.

"If you mean 'is he behaving?'...Yes he is, for now. But let's just say I have a better feeling about the changes to your father's character than I do about the changes to your Uncle Tom's!"

She smiled cheerily. She had put up with her husband for years and his problems were his own as far as she was concerned.

"Well young lady, I need to be getting on I'm afraid."

"Of course, I've got a few things to pick up in town anyway." Becky stood up to go. "Oh, I almost forgot. I got you a little something, I hope you like it."

Becky handed her the scarf.

"My dear it's beautiful!"

They said goodbye and Becky made her way out of the courtyard and around to the road. Uncle Tom was just pulling the carriage up at the front of the Inn with Mr Hamilton inside. Becky waved to her uncle. Mr Hamilton also saw her and jumped down from the carriage to speak to her.

"Welcome home young Miss Bailey," he greeted.

"Good morning Mr Hamilton," she replied, a little overwhelmed that he had come over to speak to her.

"I trust you enjoyed your visit with my sister and her family?"

"I did thank you, Sir," she replied. "I had a wonderful time."

"Well I'm very glad to hear it. I know you've helped Emma a lot over the past few months."

Becky didn't know how to reply. She just stood and smiled nervously at him.

"Well, I have to get on. Give my regards to your father."

Becky said goodbye and he carried on inside.

'Such a nice man,' Becky thought to herself as she made her way towards the Cross and then down towards the High Street.

Yes, it was lovely to be back home.

7

The festive season passed by quietly and calmly at the little lockhouse. Much to Becky's surprise, her father continued to spend time with her in the evenings and she was beginning to enjoy to the new relationship that was developing between them.

Away from the activities and noises of the main town, Becky slept peacefully while the New Year arrived and when she awoke on the first morning of 1861 she looked out of her window and had a pleasant surprise. Everything outside was covered in a thick layer of snow. She quickly dressed and went downstairs. Putting on her boots and a pulling a hat onto her head, she opened the back door and then went out to collect the eggs.

Becky loved snow. It gave her a magical sort of feeling when her feet dropped silently into the white powdery carpet which covered the back garden. Everything was so soft and tranquil. Fidget gave a faint 'meow'. He had followed Becky outside of the house and was now stood with his paws sinking into the cold snow. She laughed and clicked her tongue at him, encouraging him to be brave and follow her further into the icy wilderness. The hens were still tucked up cosily in the coop. They seemed reluctant to venture out and explore the wintry landscape that awaited them. Becky opened the coop and left some grain in the feeder for them before collecting the five warm eggs that they had laid overnight. She then made her way back to the house and started preparing breakfast.

Becky had just finished cooking the eggs when her father came in. He took off his big overcoat and went over to the dresser to fetch a plate and cup for them both. Becky served up the breakfast and they sat down together to eat.

"Are you going to go and play in the snow," he asked.

Becky smiled. It was still a little bit of a shock each time he spoke to her like this.

"Yes, I'd like to. I just don't know what to do really," she replied, hoping he might decide to come and play with her.

"Well most children tend to go sledging when it snows," he said, not understanding what she was trying to hint at.

"But I don't have a sledge."

"Oh. I see."

Having finished his breakfast, he put his knife and fork down neatly on his plate. "Well, it's quiet on the lock for a moment. I'm sure we can find some odd bits of timber somewhere and put something together for you."

"Really?!" Becky couldn't believe that he was about to make her a sledge.

"Of course."

He got up and went outside. Becky hurriedly cleared away the dishes, put on her hat, scarf and her warmest coat and went out to join him.

He had found some planks and other bits of timber in the outhouse and was already cutting and hammering nails in here and there. She tried to be helpful while at the same time not wanting to be in his way in case she might irritate him. But she had forgotten that he was a different sort of person now. He didn't get annoyed or agitated with her being around him while he worked. She could see that slowly his creation was beginning to look like a sledge. Sitting down inside the outhouse, she watched him. After a while he spoke.

"Rebecca, I've been thinking. How would you like to go to school?"

His back was to her so he would never know the expression on her face. Her jaw dropped open and her lips trembled as she struggled to respond.

"Do...do...you really mean it? You want *me* to go to school?"

Worried that he had upset her, he stopped what he was doing and turned to face her.

"I think it would be good if you could learn to read and write and that. Don't you?"

Becky jumped up. "Yes. Of course I do. I've always wanted to go to school. I just never thought you would send me."

She stood next to him, clasping her hands together with excitement.

"Thank you...Thank you."

She desperately wanted to hug him.

He knew he should reach out to her, *'It's what any normal father would do,'* he thought. *'Just step forward and put your arms around her,'* he told himself.

He held his breath and went to take a step towards her.

"Becky!!" Amy came flying around the corner before he got any further.

Jim Bailey quickly turned back to his work on the sledge and Becky greeted her friend.

"Amy, I was hoping you would come by."

Amy had entered the garden in her usual loud, brash manner. Seeing that Becky's father was there she altered her tone.

"I've been up for hours," she said, her voice hushed now so as not to annoy Mr Bailey. "I helped father and David with the milking. Then I got tired of waiting around so I grabbed my sledge and came in to find you."

Jim Bailey looked round at her. Amy opened her mouth, ready to apologise for disturbing him but it was he who spoke first.

"How is your father Amy?"

Amy's wide eyes blinked twice before she replied, "He's fine thank you Mr Bailey."

"And his new business of milking is going well is it?"

"Yes. It's going very well indeed."

"Please give them my regards." He continued hammering nails along the base of the runners for the sledge.

With his back to them Amy opened her mouth wide and mimed an over exaggerated '*what?!*' to her friend. Mr Bailey had never spoken civilly to her before. He'd only ever grunted and told her to be quiet. She'd heard people talking about the change in his character and Becky had told her about how different he was towards her but this was the first she had experienced of it. She couldn't quite believe it.

Becky smiled and shrugged, amused at Amy's shock.

"Father's just making me a sledge. I'll be ready to go in a minute."

Again, out of sight behind the man's back Amy's arms were gesturing and her mouth was opening and closing in amazement that Becky's father was *making* her a sledge.

"Actually, I think Rebecca is ready to go now."

He stood up and handed her the newly constructed sledge. It didn't look as neat and tidy as one you might buy but Becky thought it was brilliant.

"Thank you Father," she said and took it from him.

The two girls left the lock, both carrying their sledges, made their way up past the Cross and headed out of town. Other children with sledges were doing the same thing. They were all aiming for Crouch Hill, the best place to sledge in the area.

Becky excitedly told Amy that her father had mentioned sending her to school just before she had arrived at the lockhouse that morning.

"Becky, I'm so happy for you," said her friend, linking arms affectionately with her.

Becky smiled. Of all people, Amy knew just how much it meant to Becky that she was now enjoying a normal relationship with her father.

They reached Crouch Hill. There were children on sledges everywhere. Squeals of delight could be heard as girls and boys of all ages whizzed past them down the long slope. Amy and Becky climbed the hill, keeping an eye out for any out-of-control sledges that may come hurtling towards them. When they reached the top they took a moment to catch their breath and then positioned themselves so they were aiming downhill away from anyone who was walking back up. They both sat down and then counted together.

"One...two...three...go!"

With a push they lifted their legs up off the ground and both flew down the hill screaming and laughing loudly. Amy's sledge was faster but it veered off to the right and Amy desperately yelled at people to move out of her way. Although slower, Becky's sledge was well balanced and she had a lovely clear, straight run down the hill. At the bottom, neither girl knew how to stop so they just threw themselves off one side and landed in the cold, soft snow. Laughing out loud they picked up their sledges and climbed the hill for a second run.

After the fourteenth time of going up and down the hill they decided that they were tired and that it was time to call it a day. Amy could get home quicker by heading across to the small hamlet of Easington so they said goodbye and both made their separate ways home.

As Becky dragged her sledge along the, now slushy, snow she felt tired. Others were also making their way back along the road to Banbury now. She passed a father with his small daughter along the way, and it made her think of poor Mr Hardy and little Isabelle. She felt sad for a moment. Then her thoughts went to her own father and herself. She turned around briefly to look again at the child she had just passed. Becky's mother had already died when she was about the age that the little girl was. Becky's father had never taken her out to play in the snow as this girl's father was now doing. She paused in her stride, pondering over this. Then she glanced down at her funny little sledge and felt a small wave of warmth pass through her. All parents were different, she decided. Some wore their hearts on their sleeves; others were more discreet. Some played with their children; others provided them with a home and stability. Life would be boring if everyone was the same. She didn't care how she had felt in the past, she felt happy now and that was all that mattered.

8

Becky woke up feeling sick. The nerves were churning around and around in her stomach. Today was her first day at school. Her father was paying for her to attend lessons two mornings a week in classes that were being held in St Paul's Church hall, and being run by the church group.

Becky had washed and pressed her smartest dress and carefully brushed all the dirt and marks off her coat. She made her father his breakfast but felt too sick to eat anything herself. She sat and watched while he ate.

"Do you have your new notebook and pencil that I bought you?"

"Yes, thank you," she replied.

"What's wrong, don't you want to go to school?"

Despite all his efforts towards Becky he still found himself unable grasp the art of how to discern emotions in others. Becky looked at him, her face pale from anxiety.

"No Father. I do," she assured him. "It's just that I'm a little nervous. I'll be meeting new people, and I don't know if I'll be any good at the lessons."

"You'll do fine," he said, putting his empty plate by the

sink.

She nodded glumly. He walked over and gave her a reassuring pat on the arm, still not quite able to bring his arms around her as he desperately knew he should.

She could tell now what the thoughts were behind his gesture and she forced a smile onto her face.

"Yes, I'll be fine. It's just first day nerves. I'll see you after lunch."

Becky wrapped her warm coat around her and headed up the canal in the direction of St Paul's. She planned to cut through some of the back alleys north of the town centre and so avoid the busy morning bustle in town. As she made her way through the narrow streets she began to think it would have been easier to walk the usual way. These back areas were just as busy and it was harder to pass people in the small, cramped spaces. Looking back at a mother struggling with a baby in a pram to get through, she almost bumped into a gentleman coming her way. She glanced up to apologise and saw that it was Mr Hardy.

"Well, good morning young Becky, it's a pleasure to see you."

Becky stuttered, "H...he...hello Sir."

This was the first time that she had seen either Mr or Mrs Hardy since her return from London. She had not purposely avoided them but at the same time she had also not gone out of her way to visit them. Becky felt awkward. She hadn't a faintest idea what she should say.

Sensing her unease, as he had sensed with many people over the past few weeks, he continued conversation as normal.

"How was your trip to London? I hope you had a fantastic time."

Becky stopped stuttering.

"I did, thank you. I was wonderful," she paused. "Mr Hardy how are you and Mrs Hardy? I mean...I'm sorry that I didn't come by, it's just that..."

She looked down at the ground, not knowing how to go on. Tears were gathering in her eyes and her cheeks were flushing red against the cold air.

He kindly interrupted her, "Becky, it's okay."

He gently touched her elbow and she looked back up at him. He had tears in his eyes too.

"Mrs Hardy and I are getting along okay. We have good days and bad days."

Becky nodded, biting her lip. "Will you send her my regards."

"I shall. And if you have time Becky, pop by the yard and see us. Mrs Hardy would like that. You know *she* was ever so fond of you Becky."

Becky said goodbye, promising to call by in a day or two. She knew the last comment had not been about how Mrs Hardy felt towards her. She knew he had been talking about Isabelle. She had been fond of the little girl too. She pulled her handkerchief out of her pocket and wiped her eyes. At least something good had come out of the whole horrible affair; it had brought her father to his senses. She would keep her promise and she would visit Mrs Hardy and maybe she would tell her that. It might comfort her to think that Isabelle hadn't died for nothing.

Becky was at the school hall now. And her worst fears were true. Amy had warned her that a lot of the children would be younger. In Amy's class she was the eldest. Amy had said it was humiliating when a child half your age could spell better than you.

As she nervously went inside she could see that there were other, much younger children there too. The reason was that by the time children reached Becky and Amy's age they had already learned enough to know how to read and write as well as how to do basic sums and their families needed them to start working. Becky and Amy were doing things back to front. They came from families who didn't need their children to work as soon as possible but, at the same time hadn't the means or the inclination to educate them when they had been younger. Then, as she was hanging her coat carefully on a hook in the entrance way she saw a brother and sister come in. He looked about twelve years old and she maybe only a year younger. She breathed a sigh of relief. It wouldn't be just her and a group of babies learning the alphabet after all.

The morning passed quickly and Becky enjoyed herself. She soon let go of her nerves and worries about not knowing anything and just enjoyed what the teacher was telling her. She felt that the teacher had a hard job. About fifteen children attended the lesson.

From what Becky understood some attended every day and others, like herself, just one or two each week. It seemed to Becky that everyone in the class was at a different level. The teacher spent the entire morning going from one student to the next explaining different things. Although Becky was the newest in the class she caught up quickly with what was going on and didn't feel that she was getting left behind too much.

She carried her notebook home, full of little things to practice, feeling a lot more happy and content than when she had set out that morning.

9

"Give us this day our...d...day...ily daily bread."

"Well done Rebecca. That was very clearly read."

It was Becky's fifth week of lessons. As always they were reading a passage from the bible.

Becky looked up around her at the cold stone walls of the church hall and her thoughts wandered to Emma's cosy bedroom in London where the stern Miss Cartwright had begrudgingly given her a few lessons all those weeks ago.

"And lead us not into ten...temp...tentap....temtapton"

One of the other students was struggling with the big new word.

"Temptation," Becky muttered under her breath. She could not really read the word either but she did know the prayer.

One of the little ones sat next to her heard her and turned wide eyed, amazed that anyone could decipher such a formidable word. Becky smiled, and whispered it again to the child.

The child's hand shot up into the air.

"Yes, Harriet, do you know what the word says."

The teacher was humouring the small girl.

"Temptation," Harriet announced proudly.

"Well, I'm very..." the teacher caught sight of Becky's glinting eyes. "Impressed," he continued, "your reading has improved beyond recognition."

When the lesson had finished the teacher pulled Becky to one side.

"Rebecca, you know you have settled very well into the class and your reading and writing is coming on very well."

Becky looked embarrassed. "Sir, I didn't....I mean, I couldn't actually read that word, I just knew what the word was supposed to be."

"I know, I didn't think you could read *that* well."

Becky tried not to show her dismay.

He continued. "Nevertheless, you are improving. Could your father possibly enrol you for more than just the two mornings that you attend now?"

"Uh, well I doubt it. But I will ask."

Becky walked home feeling pleased with herself. She was enjoying learning. Last week she had learned to do some simple additions and she had already used her new skills to add up how much money to pay in the bakers. Before she had just handed Mr Brown a bunch of coins and let him work it all out for her.

As she approached the lock it was very quiet and she

couldn't see her father outside anywhere. She made her way around the side and entered quietly by the back door. There were gentlemen's voices coming from the front room. Becky couldn't imagine who was there. The wind caught the door as she was closing it and it was forced shut with a bang. Now Becky heard a girl's voice speak, very quietly.

"Do you think that is her?"

This was a voice that Becky knew very well. With a gasp of shock she ran immediately into the front room.

"Emma?! Is that you?"

Emma was sitting on the settee, squeezed in beside her father and Mr Hamilton. She looked shy, as always, despite the broad smile which was on her face.

"What are you doing here?" Becky went over and, forcing her to stand up, gave her a hug. "I was thinking about you just this morning in my lessons. Can you believe it? I'm going to school. But never mind that, why are you here?"

Emma, still too timid to converse in a room full of people, didn't answer any of her questions. Becky turned to address Emma's father.

"Mr Jenkins Sir, I'm sorry, I didn't greet you. Hello, I'm so pleased to see you. And you too Mr Hamilton," she added, shaking both their hands.

Becky's father was sitting in his armchair, amazed at how comfortably his young daughter engaged in conversation with the two gentlemen.

"Becky, it's so good to see you," replied Mr Jenkins. "We are all here as a family to visit my brother-in-law and his wife for a few days. Well actually, we'll be here for almost two weeks."

"You mean you're here for two weeks! That's fantastic," exclaimed Becky, again facing Emma.

Emma was nodding now and smiling in agreement.

"We hope that you and Emma will be able spend as much time together as possible before we leave," Mr Jenkins continued.

"The reason we have come by today is to give you and your father an invitation," said Mr Hamilton.

"An invitation? To what?" Becky asked.

"To a small dinner party," he replied.

"A dinner party?"

"Yes. My dear brother and sister-in-law have insisted on throwing us a small party while we are here and they especially want Emma to have her friends there. This suits Mrs Jenkins and I very well as we know nobody here in Banbury, whereas our daughter became friends with quite a few people during her last visit."

"And you want *us* to attend?" Becky could not believe that she was actually being invited to a dinner party.

"Of course we do," he assured her. "As I remember,

you and Emma were promised a special party."

Becky remembered his words when she had been in London and it was true, he had promised Emma that they would have a party together. Her eyes shone brightly as she turned to face her father.

"Please say we can go father."

He looked at her. Sadly, she could see that there was no glint of excitement at this invitation in his eyes. His expression seemed almost strained, a hint of the old Jim Bailey was there, the man who avoided all social events and grumbled at everything and everyone around him. Becky detected a faint furrow in his brow and a slight tightening of the fists, something she had not seen for a few weeks now. She held her breath. Was this it? Was this the moment when the dream changed? When he changed and went back to being his old self?

Jim Bailey was fighting a war against himself. The last thing he wanted was an evening of social merriment. If he was honest with himself and self-honesty was something that he was becoming used to, he was scared. Scared of smiling and being happy. Scared of being happy without her; without Myriam. He found the guilt the hardest thing to deal with now. He felt guilty that life was continuing and that it was actually possible for life to be good and pleasant for them both. He'd always felt that if she couldn't be there then life should be awful, a mere sorrowful existence. But of course he'd come to realise that actually, that was the very last thing Myriam would have wanted. She'd want them to be happy, not to mourn her in misery forever. He knew that now, but it was taking a while for him to adjust his ideas.

He looked back into his daughter's eyes. He could see how excited she was. He could also read her apprehension as she stood there watching him. He slowly stretched his fingers out and released the fists that he had subconsciously clenched together. This didn't go unnoticed by Becky. He also took in a deep breath of air and relaxed his forehead. Becky nodded at him, gently encouraging him. He nodded back and smiled at her. Standing up, he stepped forward to shake both of the gentleman's hands.

"We'd be very pleased to attend your little party. Thank you very much for the invitation."

Becky grabbed his arm and jumped up and down for joy.

"Thank you, Father. Thank you so much."

As she jumped her face came level with his and she thought for a moment about leaning in to kiss him on the cheek. He looked at her and then looked back anxiously at the visitors. Becky knew that now was not the time for awkward affection and she released her grip on his arm.

Mr Jenkins was laughing. "Well that's wonderful news. Now if you'll excuse us Mr Bailey we intend to drive out to the Haynes farm and invite them also."

"Oooh really?" exclaimed Becky.

"Yes, young Amy is a good friend of Emma's too," he

replied. "Actually, would you like to accompany us Becky, we have the carriage."

"Of course I would, thank you."

"Well, good day Mr Bailey, thank you for having us in. We will see you Friday evening next week then."

They shook hands with Becky's father and made their way across the lock to where Tom Watkins was waiting with the carriage. Becky climbed inside with them and they drove out of town towards the Hayneses' farm.

Emma was still quiet and seemed to get more anxious as they pulled into the farm yard. Becky squeezed her hand as they stepped out and walked over to the farmhouse. Before they got to the door Mr Haynes appeared from over in the barn. He had heard the horses enter the yard and come out to see who it was. He was not very familiar with Mr Hamilton and had never met Mr Jenkins but he recognised Becky at once. His face didn't hide his surprise at all as he looked from one to another with curiosity.

"Becky?"

Mr Hamilton stepped forward.

"Good day Mr Haynes. Joseph Hamilton." Mr Hamiton shook Mr Haynes' hand. "Sorry to come uninvited. I hope we are not disturbing your work, I'm sure it's always busy running a farm."

"No, it's fine." Samuel Haynes was quiet and mild. He wouldn't have complained if they had come at an inconvenient time anyway.

By this time Mrs Haynes and Amy had come to the door to see who had arrived in the yard.

"Becky, whatever are you doing in that great big thing," she yelled before recognising Emma. "Oh, Emma it's you! Well I never..."

Hot headed and brash as ever Amy came running across to them.

Mr Hamilton introduced Mr and Mrs Haynes to his brother-in law.

"Your daughter was a great help to us last year with the potato harvest," Mr Haynes said, shaking the man's hand. "Won't you step inside for some tea please? You can't stand around in this cold yard."

"Thank you but we must get back soon, we have been gone a long time already," Mr Jenkins replied. "We have just come to give your family an invitation."

While he was telling them about the upcoming dinner party for the family and especially for Emma and her friends, David quietly walked over from the stables where he had been working. Amy was about to burst, she was struggling so hard to contain her excitement. David stood behind them and watched bemused while the three girls squealed and giggled together. They didn't realise he was there and all three of them jumped when he opened his mouth and spoke.

"*Lady Rebecca*. Look at you in your fine carriage, going to the ball."

"It's hardly a ball David!" she replied.

"No, but there will be dressing up and some dancing won't there?" Amy looked at Emma for confirmation.

Emma nodded nervously, afraid to speak in front of David.

"You see, so it's almost a ball," said Amy defiantly, "and you're invited too, we all are, so don't mock."

He grinned at his feisty little sister and her two friends. Their three expressions could not have been more different. Amy was scowling at him as though he were the meanest human on earth. Becky's eyes were glazed, her thoughts obviously far away, dreaming about the upcoming party, or probably in her imagination a grand ball. Emma was avoiding his gaze, nervously looking down at the ground and fiddling with a button on her coat.

He shook his head at them and then grinned cheekily.

"Well, I suppose we're all going to have to learn how to dance then!"

10

Becky looked at her reflection in the small mirror on her dresser and tied a pale pink ribbon into her hair. It was Friday, the evening of the dinner party. She had on a pretty pink satin dress which Emma had grown out of and brought with her especially for Becky to have. Becky felt like a princess, she had never dressed up like this for anything before.

She heard the clock chime half past four downstairs; it was almost time to leave. She wondered if her father was ready, she hadn't heard a sound from his room.

Stepping onto the small landing she could see that his room was empty so she carefully made her way down the steep, narrow little stairs, anxious not to trip or to rip her lovely new dress. The back door was open. The sun had set a few minutes earlier and she could just make out the shadowy outline her father stood outside.

"Father, it's almost time for us to leave," she said, walking over to the doorway.

"Shush." He raised his hand towards her but didn't turn around. Something in the garden was holding his attention.

Becky paused. She couldn't see anything in the dusky light. Then as she stood there, she heard something rustling somewhere in the bushes. This was followed by a loud high-pitched squeal and more rustling. Becky's father clapped his hands together.

"Come on cat!" he hissed excitedly.

"What's happening?" Becky whispered.

"I think that lazy cat of yours is finally making himself useful. It sounds like he's got a rat or something."

His voice sounded excited, almost pleased with the little black and white creature. They heard some more rustling and another loud squeal then Fidget appeared, proudly carrying his capture. It was indeed a rat, still twitching as its body was dying. Fidget went to bring his dinner inside and Becky's father quickly pushed him back out into the garden.

"No way little fella, you can keep that thing out here."

He came inside.

"Well, at last that animal of yours is proving to be worth having around..."

He stopped speaking mid-sentence. His back had been turned to Becky as he had shut the door. Now turning around to face her he was silenced and the two of them stood and stared at each other for a few moments. His breath was taken away by her appearance. She could not believe it was her father who stood in front of her in the small kitchen.

"Y...you look so different," she stuttered.

He was wearing a suit. It was his only suit, from his

wedding day. She'd never seen him in a suit before. He had on a fancy neck-tie, clean polished shoes and he'd even combed his hair. He looked handsome. He didn't look like her father, more like a young man. She smiled.

"You look good."

He gave a quick half raise of his eyebrows in acknowledgement of what she had said but he was still staring at her, mesmerised.

"You look amazing," he replied softly. "You look beautiful," he paused and then quietly added, "like an angel."

Becky blushed. She fiddled awkwardly with the lace on her little handbag. This was the first time he'd ever given her such a generous compliment. Although it was strange to hear, she liked it. It gave her a warm feeling. She could feel his eyes still staring at her. Chuckling to herself she looked back up at him.

"You look younger," she grinned.

"You look older," he smiled.

His thoughts seemed a million miles away. They were; He was wondering where all the years had gone. Wondering why he had let her childhood slip by. Here she was, looking all grown up, and he'd missed it all. He must not miss any more he thought to himself. He would not waste any more time. Then with a clap of his hands he came back to reality.

"We'd better get going then."

He helped her on with her coat and they carefully crossed the lock. Together they walked up through the town towards the Coaching Inn. As they walked, Jim Bailey looked at his daughter. With her arms swinging, she had a spring in her step. In the light of the street lanterns he could see her eyes glinting with excitement. He suddenly realised that all his apprehensions about the evening had gone. His thoughts were so focused on her and her enjoyment that he had forgotten his own anxious concerns.

He'd struggled for years to show her any affection but now he felt he was able to. He slowly reached out and gently took hold of her hand. She looked up at him in surprise as he wrapped her small, cold fingers around his and then put both of their hands into his coat pocket. She'd been waiting for this moment. She smiled and leaned against him. They walked on without talking. They didn't need to.

All too soon it seemed to Becky, they arrived at the inn and he released her hand from his. She would have happily walked to London and back if that moment could have carried on. Jim Bailey felt the same and he gave her a reassuring pat on the arm as they walked up the steps and were greeted by one of the maids who took their coats.

Becky had never been inside the front entrance of the Coaching Inn before and she was amazed by how dark the hallway seemed. Heavily panelled with wood it was an impressive entrance but seemed somewhat eerie in the evening light.

"Through this way please Miss," encouraged the maid,

as she directed them through a doorway to the personal quarters of the Hamiltons. There was less panelling through here and the lanterns on the walls seemed to shine brighter.

They were shown to the dining room where Mr and Mrs Hamilton and the others were already gathered enjoying a glass of elderflower wine. They were the last to arrive.

"My apologies if we are late," said Mr Bailey, greeting his hosts. "The cat distracted us with a catch just as we were about to leave."

"Not at all," Mr Hamilton replied. "You are perfectly on time. Now, can I get you a glass of wine?"

Jim Bailey was poured a glass and he greeted the others. It was a small party, just fourteen of them. Samuel and Mary Haynes were there with David and Amy. Emma and her father and mother were there along with Gwen and her Fiancé, Charles, Miss Cartwright was also with them and of course Mr and Mrs Hamilton.

Becky went over to where Amy and Emma were standing sipping at a small glass of the elderflower wine which they had been given. A maid brought one for Becky also.

"Mmm, it's delicious," she said, giggling that they were being allowed to have a glass of wine.

Amy and Emma were both dressed up too. Becky didn't think that Emma looked too much different from usual as she always wore nice clothes and looked smart but the transformation in Amy was unbelievable. Amy was always in work clothes with untidy hair but tonight she looked incredible. Emma had also given her a dress, a bright yellow dress with white lace. It suited Amy's flushed skin and her blonde hair hung beautifully, all brushed neatly, down her back. Becky couldn't believe she could look so pretty.

"You look wonderful Amy, so different all dressed up."

"It's frightfully uncomfortable though isn't it?!" she replied, contorting her body to fiddle with the fastening at the back of her dress.

Becky knew this was just her way of shrugging off an embarrassing compliment and shook her head at her friend. "You're enjoying being dressed up really!"

"I suppose I am," Amy admitted. She paused, "speaking of dressed up, I've never seen you're father look so good."

"I know," agreed Emma. "I hardly recognised him."

"Yes," Becky looked over at him. He was chatting comfortably with Emma's parents. "He's very different."

She wasn't going to tell them that he had held her hand and told her she was beautiful. They wouldn't understand what that meant to her. They really were part of normal families. She didn't want to seem silly to them.

"Well, look at these three lovely ladies."

David had got bored of listening to his father and mother's conversation with the Hamiltons and had come over to see what the girls were talking about.

He also looked very different wearing his finest clothes.

"I hope you'll all dance with me later," he said, beaming at them.

"All of us at once?" laughed Amy.

"Why not?!" he teased. "Either way, I'll try not to stand on any toes."

At that a bell was rung and it was time for dinner to be served. They all sat down at the beautifully laid table to enjoy the meal. The food was delicious and Becky savoured each mouthful. She knew that Aunt Rosa would have been working hard all afternoon preparing this for them.

Most of the conversation around the table was about business and adult things. The three girls listened politely but didn't find it very interesting. Then Mr Jenkins asked Becky and Amy how they were getting along with their lessons now that they had both recently started school. Amy spoke avidly about her classes and the things she was learning. Becky, a little more reserved in such a large group, commented that she also enjoyed her lessons.

"I'm sure you are getting along very well, you showed a lot of promise while you were with us in London," said Mr Jenkins and then changed the subject. "Now, David, what are your plans for the future?"

As the adults turned their attention from the girls to David, Jim Bailey looked across at his daughter with pride. This didn't go unnoticed by Mary Haynes who smiled happily at them both.

Once dinner was over they all moved to a large room which the Hamiltons used as a lounge. The chairs had been rearranged to leave an open area free at one end of the room by the piano.

"Gwen, my dear, I believe you have brought some of your music books with you?" enquired Mr Hamilton.

"Yes, I have them by the piano already," she answered.

"Perhaps when you feel ready, we could have some music so that we may enjoy a little dance."

"Of course," she replied and moved over to the piano.

After a few moments Gwen selected a lively tune and began to play. Mr Hamilton led his wife over to the cleared area and they started dancing together. Moments later they were joined by Samuel and Mary Haynes. Mr Jenkins and his wife also stood up to dance. Becky could see that she was looking much better than she had a few months ago in London and it pleased her to see them dancing.

David grabbed Amy. "Come on, you and I know this one."

Becky laughed as he dragged Amy up and spun her around.

Emma looked at Becky. "Do you remember this tune?"

Becky listened for a moment and then she remembered. "Of course, this is the one we danced to at the top of your stairway."

"Shall we?" she asked Emma.

"Won't we look silly? You know, two girls."

"No. Anyway, this is *your* party."

Giggling together they stood up and joining the others who were dancing. They whirled around and around, narrowly avoiding bumping into other couples. When the music stopped everyone clapped and caught their breath. Gwen started to play another tune. This time Charles wanted to dance with Emma. Becky went to go to sit down and watch but Mr Hamilton stopped her.

"Mrs Hamilton has gone to get a drink, may I have this dance?"

"I'm afraid I don't know this one," Becky replied.

"It's okay, I can lead you."

He took her by the hand and they began to dance together. It was less lively than the previous dance and Becky felt very grown up as they glided around the room. She smiled, happily, across her shoulder at her two friends when they passed each other.

Aunt Rosa, who had finished clearing the kitchen, had decided to have a little look at how the evening was going and was now stood leaning against the doorway to the room, discreetly out of sight. Jim Bailey spotted her and moved over to where she was standing, hiding in the shadows. She didn't look at him. Her gaze was focused on Becky. Enchanted, she watched as Mr Hamilton expertly guided her niece around the room. Becky's dark hair was styled carefully, a few curls beautifully framing her delicate face. Her pink satin dress swished to and fro as she moved gently from side to side. Her blue eyes were shining brightly, flashing and sparkling as she smiled happily at everyone around her. Her father and her aunt stood together, side by side, quietly watching her every move. It was Jim Bailey who broke the silence between them.

"She looks just like her mother."

Aunt Rosa, a little surprised by his unexpected mention of Myriam, turned to face him. "I was thinking the very same thing."

"She's such a beautiful little girl." The admiration was clear in his voice.

Aunt Rosa touched her brother-in-law gently on the arm. "Jim, she'll be fourteen this year. She's not a little girl any more."

He frowned and looked back at his daughter. Then smiling he replied, "You're right Rose, she's not a little girl. She's a young lady."

"Yes, she's a fine young lady indeed," Aunt Rosa nodded and then chuckled gently to herself.

"Why are you laughing?" he asked.

"I was just thinking," she explained. "About that little song all the children sing, the one about the Cross and the lady on the horse."

"What about it?"

Aunt Rosa took hold of both his hands in hers, looked him in the eyes and then softly began to sing,

> *"Ride a cock horse, to Banbury Cross.*
>
> *To see a fine lady, who lives by the lock.*
>
> *With a father who loves her, (that's something she knows),*
>
> *She will be happy, wherever she goes."*

He nodded, a hint of a tear in his eyes.

The song that Gwen was playing was coming to an end. They both watched as Becky gave a little curtsey and finished her dance with Mr Hamilton. Gwendoline looked through her music book for the next song she would play.

"Do you think you could still remember how to dance after all these years?" asked Aunt Rosa.

"Of course I can. Myriam and I used to love dancing together."

He looked at her, still dressed in her work clothes.

"Surely you don't think they'll let you join the party?" he asked.

She let out an exasperated sigh and raised her eyebrows at him. "As if they ever would! I wasn't thinking of you and I dancing together you fool."

He looked at her. "Oh?"

"No." Aunt Rosa indicated with a jerk of her head towards the room full of people.

Charles was sitting by the piano with Gwen. Others were getting ready for the next dance; Mr Haynes was waiting in the middle of the room with Amy. Mrs Haynes and David were also joining them. Mr Jenkins was asking his sister for a dance while Mr Hamilton was walking towards Emma.

Jim Bailey's eyes followed Aunt Rosa's movement. Becky was sitting back down, hoping to be asked for another dance. Now he understood what she had meant. Patting Aunt Rosa's hand gently, he took in a deep breath and then walked over to ask his beautiful daughter if she would like to dance.

THE END

ONE FINE LADY

ABOUT THE AUTHOR

Raised in Oxfordshire and currently residing in Essex, Abigail Shirley loves the simpler things in life. After marrying her wonderful Cornish husband, her heart fell in love with his home county and in particular Bodmin Moor.

She enjoys walking, swimming, cycling and horse riding. The perfect end to a perfect day for Abigail would be sitting by a fire with a glass of red wine and some melted marshmallows, accompanied by a few close friends.

A vivid daydreamer, her mind often drifts away and she enjoys writing short stories and quirky poems as small gifts for her family and friends.

One Fine Lady is Abigail's first novel.

Contact Abigail by email at
abigailshirleyauthor@outlook.com

Or follow on Instagram: abigailshirleyauthor

ONE FINE LADY

Printed in Great Britain
by Amazon

62364541R00180